THE BUFFALO HUNTERS

THE BUFFALO HUNTERS

TOM CURRY

**WHEELER
CHIVERS**

This Large Print edition is published by Wheeler Publishing, Waterville, Maine, USA and by AudioGO Ltd, Bath, England.
Wheeler Publishing, a part of Gale, Cengage Learning.

LIBRARY OF CONGRESS CATALOGING-IN-PUBLICATION DATA

Curry, Tom, 1900–
  The buffalo hunters / by Tom Curry.
    p. cm. — (Wheeler Publishing Large Print western)
  "A Rio Kid western"—T.p. verso.
  ISBN-13: 978-1-4104-3485-2 (softcover)
  ISBN-10: 1-4104-3485-0 (softcover)
  1. Large type books. I. Title.
PS3505.U9725B84 2011
813'.52—dc22   2010045260

BRITISH LIBRARY CATALOGUING-IN-PUBLICATION DATA AVAILABLE
Published in 2011 in the U.S. by arrangement with Golden West Literary Agency.
Published in 2011 in the U.K. by arrangement with Golden West Literary Agency.

U.K. Hardcover: 978 1 445 83644 7 (Chivers Large Print)
U.K. Softcover: 978 1 445 83645 4 (Camden Large Print)

Printed in the United States of America
1 2 3 4 5 6 7 15 14 13 12 11

THE BUFFALO HUNTERS

Chapter I
Six-Gun Persuader

"Well, Olsen, what d'yuh say?" demanded the huge hombre slouched in the armchair. "We're offerin' yuh a swell chanct to jine our Hide Syndicate."

Olsen, a slim man with hair turning gray at the temples, blinked nervously and his glance involuntarily sought the closed door at the rear of his parlor, behind which his wife and three children were sleeping.

"Now, wait, McGlone," he began pleadingly. "Look at what I've done. I've built up my bus'ness from a ten-dollar bill. I got ten thousand hides waitin' in my yard for shipment east tonight. Yuh say yuh pay me what percentage the Syndicate kin. Where's that leave me? S'pose yuh decide yuh make no profit, or jist a few cents? I got to take yore word for it —"

"Nebraska Bull" McGlone shifted impatiently. Huge of body, his crisp black hair was long under the "Nebraska" hat he wore, the flat-topped Stetson of heavy gray felt held under the jutting chin by a wide brown-leather strap.

McGlone had not shaved for several days but even when he did the wire of his beard showed blue in his tanned flesh. He sported a narrow, close-trimmed mustache. His nose was broken, its bridge lost in swollen tissue, and his small eyes were shot with red flecks caused by excessive consumption of liquor. Yet nothing could touch the physical strength of such a man, he was as powerful as a bull and as ruthless in his way. Olsen was no match for him.

McGlone's buffalo-hide jacket rustled as he moved. He sniffed, one side of his thick-lipped, sullen mouth turning up, a characteristic of his. He had on gray pants tucked into high, great black boots covered with dust. And Olsen, blinking with dread, did not miss the big six-shooters McGlone carried in supple black holsters at his wide hips. McGlone was wide all the way down and all the way around; he seemed to fill the little room.

"I've visited several independent dealers already tonight, Olsen," he snarled, "and I mean to visit more after I'm through with yuh. That don't give me much time. Here, sign this."

He whipped from his breast pocket a paper which Olsen quickly read.

"Why, this is a bill of sale for my hides, McGlone!"

"Shore, sign it, I said."

Olsen jumped to his feet.

"Now look, McGlone. I got a family to take keer of. What yuh payin' me?"

"Pay yuh what we kin. Sign, damn yuh!"

Olsen flushed red as a beet. His Colt pistol hung from a wooden peg at the back of the room; there was a Winchester there, too.

Then, as he stared past McGlone he saw something. Through the crude window glass looking out on the front veranda he escried the dark shadows of men, and one evil face, with distorted nose, pressed against the pane.

Premonition of what would happen if he did not yield, swept over Olsen. Quickly he took the pen and ink, and signed his name to McGlone's paper.

"There yuh are, I'll jine," he muttered, anxious now only to be free of the killer. Once McGlone was gone, he would appeal to the Law of Kansas, tell the truth — that he had signed his hides over to McGlone under duress.

Nebraska Bull McGlone deliberately folded the paper which transferred Olsen's hides to the Syndicate, stuffed it inside his breast pocket. He stood up, towering a foot higher than Olsen. He sniffed again, his mouth twitching.

"Look out, Olsen," he roared suddenly. "There's somebuddy aimin' a gun at yuh from the winder —"

At that instant Olsen knew he was doomed, and not from any man at the window either. He tried to fall away from the giant, but McGlone's heavy, walnut-stocked .45 six-shooter flashed out, hand expert in its use. The tendons of Bull McGlone's gunhand tautened; the pistol blared fire and death. The slug tore into Olsen's breast, ripped half his clavicle loose, driving it up into his jugular vein. Blood spurted as the stricken man began to tremble violently, mouth dropping wide open as he could no longer take air into his lungs. He crashed on the floor, but McGlone got him in the left eye before he hit the rough boards of the cottage.

With a sniff, Nebraska Bull McGlone stepped back, reaching to open the door without looking behind him. He had his eyes on the portal at the rear, from which a woman set up a sudden screaming.

Outside, the Kansas night was mild. A wind picked up the dust from the vast, encircling plains about Ellsworth, the plains where the buffalo roamed, millions on millions of shaggy beasts that furnished valuable hides, beef, fat for tallow, bones for the carbon factories.

It was late, but the many saloons and gambling palaces which faced each other, the Kansas Pacific Railroad tracks running east-and-west in the middle, were lighted up. Horses and teams stood hitched to the rails at the outer edges of the awnings.

Bull McGlone, the killer, joined his half dozen followers. Their horses were close at hand and they mounted, rode away from the frame house where Dan Olsen had lived.

Pete Tallifero, a thin, snaky looking devil whose high cheekbones and dull black eyes showed the Indian strain in him, asked a question.

"Yuh hadda shoot him, huh, Bull? Wouldn't he jine?"

"Naw. Figgered on foolin' me," growled McGlone, as he reloaded his Colt and let it slide back into its holster. "Soon as I'd gone, he meant to git the sheriff."

McGlone led the way through a gap in the houses south of Ellsworth, they rode out from the lines of buildings. At the east end, under the prairie stars, stood a darkened home. McGlone dismounted and went up on the porch. With the butt of his six-shooter he rapped loudly on the door.

A window opened. A man asked: "Who's that?"

"It's Bull McGlone, Carter. Wanta talk to yuh. C'mon down and light up."

"Why not tomorrer, Bull?" asked Carter.

"This is mighty important, Carter. Yuh got any hides on hand?"

"Jist sold my last thousand this mornin'."

"I see." McGlone looked around, gave Pete Tallifero a signal. As McGlone talked to Carter, Tallifero stealthily drew his pistol. A shot crackled in the darkness, the blue-red flare stabbing upward, and Carter, the bachelor who lived alone, fell dead on the window sill, body hanging from the opening.

"That sidewinder'd never have jined," growled McGlone as they hurried away. "He's a pal of Fred Grey's."

"What say we take Grey next?" asked a tall, broad-shouldered hombre who wore buckskin and a narrow-brimmed hat.

"Okay, Harry," McGlone shrugged. "Let's go. But remember, boys, Grey's mayor of the town. We got to make it mighty keerful, savvy?"

"Yeah, but the Chief wants him most of all," "One-Shot" Harry Crane growled. "If

12

anybuddy bucks us, Grey'll be the one."

One-Shot Harry Crane, buffalo hunter, gunman and fugitive from the justice of a dozen frontier towns from the Rio Grande to Kansas, had a level voice that was as cold as ice. He could kill with a carelessness not even equalled by McGlone. McGlone had to lash himself into a kind of rage before he drew and fired. Crane killed the way most men would light a cigarette.

The others were of similar stamp, gunmen, tough frontier characters who had indulged in many a shooting scrape. They didn't have the big reputations of the three leaders of the Hide Syndicate — McGlone, Tallifero and Crane — but they were motivated by the same desire for gain.

They swung over to the north side, away from Carter's, and were not stopped.

Gunshots were not uncommon in Ellsworth at the time. Texas men, driving thousands of cattle up the Trail to the railroad, let loose in Kansas, firing off their pistols in sheer exuberance at being rid of their troublesome bovine charges, after the long weeks of grinding drive. Quarrels were constantly developing between quick-tempered, egotistical hombres, at the gambling tables, along the many bars. And in those days everybody who carried a gun indulged daily in target practice and there were few who did not go armed at one time or another.

In its prime as a depot for Texas cattle, and for the buffalo hides and carcasses coming in by hundreds of thousands, Ellsworth hummed with the madness of the frontier — high, wide and handsome.

The next stop of the riders, after a short interlude during which a bottle of whiskey passed the rounds, was at a more pretentious dwelling which had a yard around it. Set in the main part of town, the home of Mayor Fred Grey, biggest hide dealer in Kansas, was larger than most neighboring private homes. There were white curtains at the windows and some flowerpots with plants growing in them standing outside on a shelf.

McGlone went up on the porch, standing in the shadows, big boots spread wide. He banged on the door. This place, too, was darkened for the night, those inside asleep. But this did not worry McGlone, who kept banging until a second-floor window raised.

"Who is it and what do you want?" a girl's voice demanded.

"Is yore old man home, Miss Ruth?" growled McGlone, looking up.

He could see the pale oval of the young

woman's face. McGlone knew Ruth Grey, knew how young and pretty she was. He could picture her large blue eyes and the sheen of dark hair which crowned her trim head. She had real spunk, too, thought McGlone, a girl with a way of her own. McGlone had on several occasions sought to know her better but Ruth Grey had held him at arm's length with her cool, matter-of-fact manner.

"Who are you?" Ruth asked.

"It's McGlone, Ma'am. Need to see yore dad, it's mighty important."

"Well, he's not here, Mr. McGlone. He had a call to go over to Salina on some business and won't be back till tomorrow night."

"Okay, Ma'am. Thanks," McGlone said concealing his anger.

McGlone swung, went back to his horse. He cursed.

"Grey ain't home. C'mon, we better report to the Chief."

Half a mile east of the main part of town stood a motley collection of shacks, low gambling house, saloons, tough places all, inhabited by the riffraff of the Frontier. It was known as Nauchville, or the Bottom.

As the gunnies under Bull McGlone galloped toward this hot spot, they could hear the sound of revelry, strains of violins and pianos, raucous voices of men and higher tones of girls who frequented the dancehalls. Tough as Ellsworth was itself, the decent part of the citizenry had relegated the worst of the night life to the Bottom. It was not safe for an honest man to walk the dusty road here after dark. Even in the daytime Nauchville was dangerous. In its dingy, raw-board shacks lurked killers and the lowest of the low.

McGlone jerked his black stallion to a sliding stop in front of a joint whose rude sign said: "BLUE BUFFALO." He strode through the wide door, not deigning to glance at the drunken men and women in the main room, past the bar, and into a rear passage which led him to a door. He knocked on this.

"Come in," a low voice ordered.

A man sat at a table, staring into the red center of a half-emptied bottle of whiskey. A single lamp burned on the table, but as the man slowly looked up to fix McGlone's hard face, the twin orbs glowed with a terrible hatred. Not hatred for McGlone but simply rage against the whole of humanity. The man's mouth was held taut and the muscles of his arms stiff.

McGlone sniffed. When the Chief was on one of these silent but terrible drunks, even

Nebraska Bull was afraid to get too close to him.

"What d'yuh want?" the hombre behind the table demanded. He was in a black fury and a gun lay within six inches of his hand.

"Ev'rything's okay, Chief," McGlone told him. "On'y we can't git the mayor tonight. Grey's done rode to Salina."

" 'Grey's done rode to Salina'," mocked the Chief, mimicking McGlone's exact intonation and wordage. He bent forward, knuckles whitened by his tense grip on the table edge, eyes blazing red sparks.

"You fool! How many have you taken care of tonight?"

"Four, Chief, but —"

"Grey's got more savvy than most. When he comes home he'll probably guess what's goin' on. He mustn't reach Ellsworth, understand? We've just started off. There are other towns to take care of."

McGlone blinked, then nodded.

"Oh, shore, Chief. I savvy. We'll start pronto, ketch Grey out on the prairie on his way back. He can't ride very fast, he's too heavy."

CHAPTER II
THE RIO KID HITS KANSAS

The sun was coming up to a golden yellow in the sky as two riders shoved their horses north. All about them stretched the interminable prairie ocean, the Great Plains, undulating flatlands of Kansas and neighboring states. Buffalo grass and bunch grass, short but thick and nutritious for the wandering herds, covered the dark-colored clay loam, bound it together, prevented rain and wind from picking it up and whipping it away.

At sparse intervals the tremendous reaches were broken by an isolated hill or prairie grove. There were no forests here, only fringes of woods along the stream courses, black walnut, cottonwoods, oak, and in the western sections, yucca and low cactus growths. Prairie chickens, jackrabbits, wild turkeys, ranged the land. But chiefly the huge buffalo herds subsisted on it, with Comanches, Sioux and Cheyenne Indians following their meat supply.

The south wind blew against the backs of the two horsemen. Dust stuck in a grayish coat to the animals' lower quarters, plastered on by water. It was not long since they had swum the Arkansas.

The man slightly in the lead was mounted

18

on a mouse-colored, unprepossessing looking dun, with a black stripe down its back-
bone — "the breed that never dies." Saber,
the horse, rolled a mirled eye and snorted
angrily as a big jackrabbit suddenly leaped
from under his raised hoof and skittered
across the buffalo grass.

Captain Robert Pryor laughed at his pet's
annoyance.

"Just a bunny, Saber," he remarked. "He's
shore on his way. Bet yuh can't catch him."

Pryor, known from the Mexican Border
to Kansas as "The Rio Kid," shifted his
broad-shouldered, narrow-waisted figure in
the sweated saddle, winking back at his
companion, the slim, eager-faced Mexican
lad, Celestino Mireles. Only a stripling,
Mireles had chosen to follow the Rio Kid
wherever he might go, offering him a devo-
tion that amounted to worship. The Mexican had the straight black hair and large
black eyes of the hidalgo. He wore a red
sash and bell-shaped pants, a straw sombrero with a purple-and-red band.

The Rio Kid was the ideal weight for a
cavalryman, which he had been during the
Civil War. By blood and early training in
Texas, by constant practice, he had become
one of the West's greatest horsemen. And,
as one of General George A. Custer's Union

19

Army scouts, he had become habituated to danger, had grown to look upon peril as the natural way to live.

Now he had on thick blue breeches tucked into black boots, a blue shirt under his leather vest. An Army Stetson covered his crisp, closely-cropped chestnut hair and shaded his straight nose. He kept his face clean-shaven, the skin smooth as golden bronze. His mouth was pleasant. Tiny incipient wrinkles at the corners of his lips and devil-may-care eyes, showed he was quick to smile. A genius at scouting, he had risen to the rank of captain under General Custer. He rode now with a boyish insouciance, and when death faced him he could laugh as easily as at a jest.

He was well-armed. A three-inch black-leather belt around his narrow waist supported two Army Colts. Under his shirt, crossed over his broad shoulders, rode another belt with a second brace of pistols. He could deliver twenty-four shots before reloading, not counting the cavalry carbine, a short-barreled rifle snugged in a sling under his leg, its ammunition in a belt attached to the saddle-horn.

About the Rio Kid was an air of command. A look at him impressed men. His gear, despite his long ride up from Texas, was neat, meticulously cared for. He had a passion for order, both ingrained and strengthened in the Army. There were wounds on him, wounds of battle. One, across his ribs, had healed unevenly and the scarred flesh was a barometer; it reacted differently from the surrounding tissue, to changes in weather, to danger.

To soothe Saber, Pryor hummed the dun's favorite tune, an Army classic:

"Said the big black charger to the little
    white mare,
" 'The sergeant claims yore feed bill really
    ain't fair.'
"Said the little white mare to the big black
    charger,
" 'Yuh forget, kind sir, that our family's
    growin' larger'."

Saber sniffed, settled down to the tireless, long-paced stride which he could maintain over so many miles. In all his experience, the Rio Kid had never ridden against another horse that could overtake the dun. Saber's appearance fooled men. He was rather bony and did not look nearly as fast as he was. He had a terrible temper with everyone save his master, acting the wild, evil mustang, lording it over other horses, allowing no one but Pryor to touch him unless implicitly instructed.

The shaggy-coated, pink-brown pinto mustang ridden by Celestino Mireles, was well aware of Saber's domineering traits and refused to stay on the line with the dun. When Saber grew irritated he was likely to reach over and bite.

"That Pembroke herd we had to ride around, Celestino," the Kid remarked, turning in his saddle to speak, "was a right big spread."

They had had to swing miles eastward of the Texas Trail. There were cattle herds coming up the Trail, and the steers must not be stampeded. Besides, the air near a traveling herd was not fit to breathe.

Pryor looked ahead, alert, eyes rising.

"Huh," he grunted. "Hear that, Celestino?"

"*Si,* General. Gunshots."

The Mexican youth, since Pryor had snatched him from death at the hands of the red raiders of the Rio Grande, who had massacred the boy's father and immediate family, insisted on calling Pryor "General."

22

To Mireles, Pryor was the general, his leader.

They searched the rolling prairie ahead. Dust whorls showed but they might be made by running cattle, buffalo — or simply the wind picking up dirt. Yet Saber sniffed, eyes rolling in pleasure — the dun loved a fight and would run toward gunshots if permitted. He shivered a warning with his black spinal stripe.

The Kid and Celestino Mireles had ridden this Trail on another occasion. They had helped blaze a new branch from west Texas to assist the pioneers of Rose Valley. Now, restless, unable to stay in one place after the excitement of the Civil War, and the murder of his parents on the Rio, the Kid sought new worlds to conquer. He had made friends in Kansas, Wild Bill Hickok, Wyatt Earp, Buffalo Bill, and others.

The railroads, coming through, steadily pushing west despite the Cheyennes and Sioux, made Kansas the great Mecca. Texans drove their beef cattle here, buffalo hunters brought in their valuable hides for sale. Kansas was booming.

With Indians roving the plains, with the many outlaws and shady characters who leeched in the cattlemen and others, it behooved a man to watch where he rode in the early 'Seventies.

As he pushed the dun on, Pryor loosed the buckle and strap of his carbine, so as to have it ready — it had a longer range than his revolvers.

The rise of the prairie cut them off for a time, although they could hear the gunshots clearer now. If it was Indians, they would avoid or outride them.

"Head for that little prairie grove," Pryor called back.

A mile ahead of them was one of the small patches of trees and rocks affording a slight relief from the monotony of the land sea, like an oasis of palms in the sandy desert. It was not more than a hundred yards across, but as Pryor and Mireles came up, they could sit their horses behind it and look out across the rolling plain.

Now they could make out what was going on. Mounted men were racing over the flat, dust spurting up from the flying hoofs of horses. The riders had their heads down, Stetsons against the wind of speed. The spurts of flame from their pistols, which they fired at a lone man out in front, were visible to the Rio Kid and his comrade.

"We'd have heard that sooner but the wind was wrong," muttered Bob Pryor.

The man out ahead of the six was not

wasting any time in turning to shoot. He was pressing his dappled gray to the full, spurs digging in, urging the animal on.

"Pairhaps, General, a shereef's posse chases an outlaw," suggested Mireles.

The Kid shook his head. "If yuh notice," he growled, "them gents in back have their bandannas up. 'Tain't for dust, I reckon. I don't see no badges on any of 'em."

His narrowed eyes took in the giant on the great black stallion who rode in the lead of the half dozen. He noted the "Nebraska" hat, the power of the big fellow. And the man running away from them he could see more and more clearly. Evidently the fugitive had spied the prairie grove some time before and hoped to reach it with the idea of using it as a haven to stand his pursuers off.

Bent low over the gray, the fleeing man glanced over his shoulder. His attackers were gaining on him. He spurred frantically on. But he was heavy, middle-aged. He could not ride with the abandon of youth and his weight deterred the mount, already tired when the race began.

"I'm goin' to see what's what, Celestino," Pryor said, and started the dun forward, galloping from cover.

At sight of him the stout man on the gray

was startled. He swerved, but seeing the Rio Kid's arm raised in a gesture of friendship, came on. They were still some distance on from the grove when the big man on the black, firing one pistol after another, hit the dappled gray with a lucky one — at such jolting, tearing speed, aim was difficult. The gray crashed instantly, and the rider hardly had time to get his feet from the stirrups. He was flung head over heels rolling like a tumbleweed ball for several yards before he brought up against a little mound, a prairie dog's burrow.

The Rio Kid reached him ahead of the pursuers. The man lay quiet, stretched on the grassy dirt, stunned by his fall. The Rio Kid, calculating his chances, fired two shots over the heads of the oncoming gunmen. They slowed, began shooting, cursing at him.

A bullet from the big fellow's pistol spat into the grass an inch from Pryor's boot as he leaped, bending over the unconscious man. A swift glance told the Rio Kid that this person was a decent citizen. He did not have the appearance of a criminal and the closer the others came, the less the man from Texas liked their looks.

Then the Kid felt the bite of a slug that tore a groove in his black belt. It burned his

26

flesh, shrieked on to bury itself in dirt. They meant business, and, bunched together around their leader, threw up their guns for a volley. No longer moving at high speed, they would be dangerous, aim better —

The Rio Kid had to give up his idea of picking up the stunned fugitive. Instead, feet wide, in a half crouch, he whirled and began shooting at them. His first shot, from the Army Colt, took one of them in the shoulder, piercing between arm and collarbone. The blood spurted from the hole, and the hombre shrieked, twisted to one side with pain.

The volley from their guns, disturbed at the psychological moment by the Kid's hit, was low. It plugged into the dirt in front of the Rio Kid and the man he sought to snatch from death. An instant later, almost echoing the concerted guns, Celestino Mireles fired a rifle from the grove and the huge hombre in the lead jumped in his leather, nipped by the boy's lead.

The Mexican lad's rifle bullets worried the attackers. They knew what they were, could distinguish the different timbre as Celestino pumped long ones their way. They turned, galloped out of range, and paused, sitting their horses to see what happened.

Pryor got the heavy man up onto his knee,

hoisted him to Saber's back. The gang had rifles, were unshipping them for a long-range duel. The Kid leaped up behind the stunned man. Saber, looking back and snorting, wicked eyes rolling in excitement, wanted to return and fight it out.

"Not till we git this feller under cover," the Rio Kid muttered grimly.

Moving as fast as possible, he shoved the dun to the prairie grove. Mireles was shooting his Winchester rifle at the gang of gunnies. Long bullets were traded back and forth. Saber made the grove, swung around out of sight behind the trees.

Celestino kept the pot boiling as the Kid lowered the heavy-set man to earth. The fugitive's hair was gray at the temples, pepper-and-salt on top, shaggy as a buffalo's. He had a wide black mustache, a strong chin, deep-set eyes. He was about the Rio Kid's height but was forty pounds heavier, wore a black suit, neatly kept save for the fresh dust and the dirt ground in from his fall, white shirt with black string tie, and a heavy gold watch chain with an elk-tooth fob. His black hat had come off when he crashed, strap snapping. His gun-belt was nearly empty, and this told the Kid he had been on the run from the gang for some miles.

Catcalls and howls came up from the angry throats of the gunnies. Their rifle bullets were plunging blindly into the grove, seeking for them. The slugs hit trees with dull thuds or ricocheted from the rocks with shrieking whirs.

As the Kid shoved some water from his canteen in between the man's half-open lips, the latter grunted and then opened his eyes.

"How yuh feel, Mister?" inquired the Kid.

"Ugh — not so good. Bad jolted — say, yuh saved me from them rascals?"

"Sort of, I reckon. What's their game?"

"Huh? Yuh got me. Mebbe they figgered I had some money on me, since I rode over to Salina. What's yore handle, young feller?"

"Pryor, Bob Pryor. Some call me the Rio Kid."

"I'm Mayor Fred Grey of Ellsworth. I know some of them dawgs out there. That big feller's Nebraska Bull McGlone. There's Pete Tallifero with him. That snaky devil, he's an Injun breed. The one in buckskins is One-Shot Harry Crane."

"They seem all-fired anxious to set yuh at rest," drawled the Kid.

He straightened, for the riders had spread out and were forming a circle about the grove.

"Git the hosses in among the trees, Celestino," he ordered. "We'll take to the rocks. Looks like we're in for a little siege."

Fred Grey took a long drink from the proffered canteen. "Gimme a gun," he said, "and I'll do my bit, Rio Kid. I'm much obliged."

The trio flattened out in the rocks, Pryor rolling a couple into better protective position. He began to fix himself a cigarette.

"Say, yuh're a nervy one, Kid," Mayor Grey remarked admiringly. "Yuh don't seem excited. Where was yuh bound, anyways?"

"Was headin' to hook up with Wild Bill Hickok — he offered me a marshal's job when I was in Kansas last time."

"Huh? Yuh'll have trouble findin' Hickok right now — 'leastways, Gen'ral Custer has. Bill got in a scrape at Hays with three of Custer's soldiers, and he took it on the run. Bill got 'em all, and 'twasn't his fault, but he figgered dustin' was best. It's rumored he's gone on the stage with Buffalo Bill Cody in the east."

"I rode under Custer in the war," the Rio Kid drawled. "Is the Gen'ral around now?"

"Nope, he's way off west after some Sioux. Say, we better git our guns busy, them fellers're behavin' right bold."

"Zey mean to start fire, General," Mireles

30

cried suddenly.

Bull McGlone, face masked to his fierce eyes, had got down from his horse, some distance to the south, while his mates kept up a hot fusillade at the prairie grove. The grass was rustling dry in the wind. A little blaze started would roar swiftly into the grove, smoke them out —

With a curse, Pryor seized his carbine, fired at McGlone, but the range was too long. He saw the crimson flames leaping with the wind, the rising smoke.

"We'll hafta ride west out of it," he growled.

Chapter III
Friends in Need

Had it not been for the necessity of protecting Mayor Fred Grey, there would have been little difficulty. Grey's horse lay dead north of the prairie grove. Saber might carry double for a time but Grey was a heavy man and the dun could not make his usual speed with such a load on his back.

The Rio Kid had to make his decision fast. The grass-fire was whipping toward them on the fresh south wind and the horses, Celestino's pinto and the dun, were growing alarmed, sniffing at the smoke, beginning to dance. Wild by nature the mustangs would not face a fire.

Pryor grasped Saber's bridle, the dun pushing his velvet nose against his master's arm, dancing in a circle in eagerness to gallop from the threatening flames.

"Celestino — take Grey on yore horse, and start west. I'll stay behind yuh and keep 'em off."

As the light Mexican youth, guiding the paint horse, with Grey hanging on, burst full-speed from the grove, a howl of triumph rose from the gunnies. Shots began hunting them in the hot, dry air.

The Rio Kid, swinging a blue-clad leg over the dun's back, turned in his leather, and began using his carbine, meanwhile riding parallel behind the line of burning buffalo grass. The three were hardly out of the grove before the fire whipped into it, eating up dry leaves, running up tree trunks, burning dry grass and rubble. The grove was lost in a smoke cloud, and the fire was driven on, its margins slow to spread with the breeze behind it. It would run to the Smoky Hill River, a few miles north, where it should burn out, unless a shift in the wind turned it.

Soon out of the smoke area, shoving

northwest at an angle, with Bull McGlone frantically endeavoring to take them, the running battle proceeded. A gunny in their way fled before the barking carbine of the Kid. The gunmen dared not approach too close to that deadly rifle. McGlone, Tallifero and Crane were still riding, shooting, but behind lagged a fifth man, while the sixth lay stretched on the plain, a bullet from Pryor's Winchester in his brain.

But Celestino's pinto was slowing. He could not maintain a fast pace with the double weight he carried. The Kid was fifty yards to the rear, keeping the furious Mc-Glone from his prey. Apparently Nebraska Bull, aware that Grey must have recognized him, was determined to finish the mayor in order to save himself from trouble later on.

The sun beat down with a terrible, relentless heat. Suddenly the paint horse stumbled, staggered a few paces, fell, throwing Grey and Mireles to the dusty ground. The lithe Mexican lad landed like a panther, on his feet. Grey rolled over and stopped, sat up, rubbing dirt from smarting eyes.

The horse, overtaken by a rifle bullet from McGlone, quivered in the hot sun. Nebraska Bull was sure of his quarry now. The Rio Kid, shooting at the gunnies, realized it would only be a question of minutes until the unhorsed pair would be struck. His blue eyes, trained in military strategy during the war, sighted the small depression a short distance away. He had seen hundreds of them, knew it was a buffalo wallow, edges crumpled down by the heat and erosion. At some previous time a buffalo bull had lowered his shaggy head, dug in one horn, and pushing around in a circle, had cut himself a place in which to wallow.

"Git in there, boys," the Kid ordered quickly, "and keep yore heads down."

Grey and Mireles rolled into the dip. By lying flat their bodies were below the level of the prairie, and the "chug-chug" of the bullets whipping at them told that the slugs were ploughing earth.

The Rio Kid felt Saber leap under him. The dun cursed in horse language as a bullet bit a chunk of hide from his flank, blood dripping in its path. The Kid had to make a quick decision: either he must ride out of bullet range or he must send the dun out of it alone. If he left, it would mean deserting Grey and his Mexican pal.

McGlone paused to speak to the wounded gunny, who appeared from the southeast. Pryor leaped from his saddle, ordered: "Git out of it, Saber." He slapped the dun's ribs and Saber flew from the spot. He would come when the Rio Kid called him. The Kid threw himself into the buffalo wallow, squeezing between Grey and Celestino.

Now the wounded hombre to whom McGlone had spoken took a northeast course away from the spot.

"Gone to fetch help," growled Fred Grey.

The Rio Kid, eyes slitted under his Stetson brim, dust caking his bronzed face, nodded. McGlone spread his men out, covering all sides of the wallow, but they stayed back out of rifle range.

Two hours passed. McGlone was simply holding them there until he brought in more fighters.

"How far's Ellsworth?" asked the Kid.

"Oh, a fast horse kin make it in an hour and a half or so."

They lay low, conserving ammunition for the last stand. The ominous horsemen sat facing them, guns ready. The afternoon was getting on when Mireles indicated a dust cloud approaching from the north.

"They're comin'," agreed Grey.

The Rio Kid had his carbine and pistols loaded. About them lay the baked, undulating ocean of prairie. Eastward, the grove was a blackened ruin against a smoky blue sky. The grass fire had quickly burnt itself out when it reached the Smoky Hill River.

"Someone comes from west, too, General," muttered Celestino Mireles.

The Rio Kid, who had been watching the dust cloud from the north, swung to stare in the direction Mireles indicated. The wind was picking up other dust that way and from the west presently showed a party of horsemen, a dozen and a half riding in a compact group. In sight, too, were McGlone's aides, led by the wounded lieutenant.

But Nebraska Bull saw the approaching party from the west. Black rage seized him and he began to curse, shooting futilely at the men in the buffalo wallow.

"They're buffalo hunters," cried Fred Grey.

Rapidly the party of hunters approached, drawn perhaps by the smoke seen in the sky earlier, and now by the crack of guns. Nebraska Bull McGlone threw his hand high, signaling his men off. They rode a wide circle to evade the snapping guns of the Rio Kid, and galloped away in a dust cloud. They headed off the dozen gunnies from Ellsworth, the two groups merged and galloped townward, disappearing behind the dip in the prairie.

The Rio Kid stood up, grinning. He whistled shrill blasts of "Said the Big Black Charger," and presently Saber's mouse-colored shape came whirling to him. He sprang into his saddle, rode toward the hunters, hand held high in a gesture of peace and welcome.

The men coming toward him were lean-faced hunters of the plains. At their head rode a lithe young man, corn-colored down pencilling the outline of a mustache on his upper lip, light blue eyes hard as jade in the sunlight. In years a boy, yet on the frontier the child passed into manhood through no intervening stage; life was too severe to allow coddling. As the Rio Kid came up he recognized the youth on the dusty buckskin.

"Howdy, Bat!" he sang out.

He had met Bat Masterson on a previous trip to Kansas. William Barclay Masterson, few of years though he was, had already made a great name for himself among the courageous, hardy plainsmen. Quick of eye, stealthy of foot, steady of hand, he had reminded old-timers of one Batiste Brown, celebrated hunter of the days of Bridger, Sublette and St. Vrain, and from this had come his nickname by which everybody knew him — Bat.

"Why, it's the Rio Kid!" cried Bat Masterson. "How's the man from Texas?"

Artistic by nature, Bat indulged this flair in his dress. The bandanna about his bronzed neck was of red silk. His steel spurs were inlaid with gold. His gray sombrero was circled by a braided bullion band of gold and silver worked into the shape of a rattlesnake, fanged and with red eyes of glass. Bat had paid one hundred buffalo robes for this hatband.

About his slim waist was a crimson sash, fringed ends hanging past his thigh. His saddle was of stamped leather, expensive as they were made, his warbags and leggings faced with dogskin that would shed rain. The only thing plain about his gear was the .50 caliber Sharps rifle, named Marie, under his buckskin-covered leg. Heavy, eight-square, it was entirely for business reasons.

"Here, Houston, here, yuh old devil," Bat soothed his favorite mustang as Houston bit back at Saber, who had taken a chunk of hide from the buckskin first. "Say, Kid, keep that consarned gray imp of Satin in order, will yuh? Houston ain't the sort to take an insult from any hoss."

Masterson introduced the Rio Kid to the rest of the hunters.

"Meet Bob Pryor, known as the Rio Kid, boys. He's a good friend of Wyatt Earp's. When I seen him fust down in Oklahoma he had a couple hunderd of Virgil Colorado's Injuns on his tail. I shore was impressed that day, Kid, by yore choice of followers." Bat grinned under his downy mustache, then grew serious as he named the hunters with him.

"This here's Vern Burnett, Pryor."

Vern Burnett was about Bat's age. He was tall, broad through the chest, weighing around 180 pounds. Curly hair, bleached by the hot sun, showed under his dark Stetson. He had keen brown eyes, somber as a lion's. About him was the gravity of an old man, despite his youth. He, too, carried a Sharps .50 caliber buffalo gun, besides a walnut-stocked Colt revolver, Frontier Model, at his waist. His face was rather long, with a square chin, his cheekbones prominent in the deeply-tanned flesh.

The Rio Kid put him down instantly as a strong man, and a good one to have with you in a fight. The fellow's hands were big, showed the effects of hard toil; his halfboots were thrust into nickel-plated stirrups on the heavy chestnut stallion he mounted. His buckskin jacket was open to his breastbone, matted with hair, hide-bronzed as his face.

Another hunter pressed forward, older, smiling good-naturedly at Bob Pryor.

"This here's Jim Hanrahan, the wust rascal nawth of the Red River," Masterson said solemnly, but with an intonation revealing that Hanrahan was one of Bat's best pals. "Bermuda Carlisle," went on Masterson, indicating each buckskin-clad hunter as he named him, "Billy Ogg, Mike Welch, Old Man Keeler, Billy Dixon, Cheyenne Jack, Andy Johnson, Kansas Hendry —" There were a dozen-and-a-half bronzed plainsmen with Masterson.

Introductions over, they rode on to the spot where Fred Grey and Celestino Mireles stood. Grey sang out greetings to them all. They knew him, had sold hides to him. Quickly Grey told them of the attack made on him by Nebraska Bull McGlone and his crowd.

"Yuh boys scairt 'em off," Grey said. "I reckon drinks're on me. Let's head for Ellsworth."

The buffalo hunters had spare horses with them, so Mireles and Grey were able to ride.

"What brought yuh nawth ag'in, Kid?" asked Bat as they trotted their horses toward Ellsworth.

"Sorta thought I might find Wild Bill Hickok," replied Pryor. "But Grey says he's took it on the run, 'count of some shootin' scrape he was in."

"Yeah, that's so, him'n Custer had some trouble. But why don't yuh come buffalo huntin' with us? We're plannin' a big hunt, down in the Panhandle. 'Dobe Walls is our headquarters."

"No, sir," cried Grey. "I'll tell yuh what I mean to do, boys, and that's pin a marshal's star on this Rio Kid! He's the sort of officer we need in Ellsworth. The town's got outa hand and it'll take a feller like Pryor to calm her down. I mean to make Bull McGlone and his pals pay for what they done to me. Must be some reason behind it."

Chapter IV
Ellsworth

Light was still over the plains as they came to Ellsworth town. Smoke hung heavily in the sky, woodsmoke from dozens of the trail driver camps. Out from the city the cowboys held their herds until the great area of loading pens along the K.P. tracks could accommodate them or a buyer might be found. On the sidings stood lines of cattle cars. The distant bellowings of thousands of steers confused the smoky air.

The Rio Kid looked over the roaring cowtown for the first time. He had seen Abilene and there were some similarities. But Ellsworth had been built along the railroad tracks, east and west. The main street was extremely wide, the steel road splitting the town in half. There were no trees, no bush growth. Laid out in '67, the Smoky Hill had overflowed and put the town under four feet of water, washing away many frail buildings. This had forced the citizens to move to higher ground, but Indians and cholera had discouraged the population, which dwindled to less than fifty.

After a year, however, a second growth, mushroom in character, took place. Texas cattle-trade shifted to Ellsworth and the permanent population swelled to around a thousand, although in summer and fall, with the herders, there were two or three times that many.

North Main Street was above the tracks, South Main below. The business section ran for three or four blocks, one or two-story frame structures, with verandas facing the railroad. Here and there showed a brick building, Minnick and Hounson's drug store on South Main, Larkin's Hotel on North, the courthouse and jail a block east of Larkin's. Board sidewalks lined the earthen streets, a foot deep in mud when it rained, although in front of his hotel Larkin had constructed a stretch of stone sidewalk, the pride of Ellsworth. Benches were under the wooden awnings for the pleasure of loafers, whittling in the shade. Hitch-racks were filled, day and night, with teams or cow ponies.

The party of buffalo hunters, with Grey, Mireles and the Rio Kid, cut through a side street and hit South Main. Town was crowded, with cowmen, beef buyers, gamblers, hunters, dealers and riffraff. Pryor could identify many of the buildings by the crude signs out front — a three-story hotel, the Drover's Cottage, which had 84 rooms, Jake New's Saloon; Kelly's American House; Nick Lentz' which advertised not only whiskey but hot and cold baths; Beebe's General Store, Brennan's Saloon, with the railroad station opposite Beebe's.

The new courthouse and lock-up were on the north side of the tracks two blocks east of Douglas. The Grand Central Hotel, where Buffalo Bill Cody, Wild Bill Hickok, Wyatt Earp, Ben and Bill Thompson, and other famous westerners stopped at one time or another, was at the corner of Lincoln and Main. Nagel's Livery Stable, and a dozen more saloons and gambling halls, made up the more notable structures.

The stockyards were at the west of town, some distance along the tracks, made of raw lumber whitewashed in haste, and covering acres of ground. Two hundred cars of cattle a day could be shipped from Ellsworth. On the grassy plains were more herds, and Texas men, the Civil War and Reconstruction rankling in their bold hearts, strove to make life at least interesting and exciting for the northern marshals.

Celestino Mireles stared with interest at the sights of the roaring cowtown. Ellsworth had as wild-and-woolly a reputation as any settlement in Kansas. Dust hung heavy in the air, and thousands of steers formed an obligato to the shriller sounds of carousing men and girls.

The party of hunters walked their horses past a yard in which were stacked piles of buffalo hides as high or higher than the houses.

"That's Olsen's store yard," explained Bat Masterson to the Rio Kid. "Hide bus'ness is boomin'. Yuh better make that run to the 'Dobe Walls on the Canadian with us, Pryor. Yuh kin git five dollars apiece for good hides and the Cheyennes ain't bin ornery lately."

"I'm for the hide bus'ness, bein' in it myself," drawled Fred Grey. "But the way things look, Bat, I'd ruther have the Rio Kid nearer my pusson than the Panhandle! Here's my place, c'mon in and squat."

Most of the hunters, having seen Grey safely home, said *adios* and scattered through the town, hunting amusement and food. But Captain Pryor, Mireles, Vern Burnett and Bat Masterson, followed the heavy-set Grey around back of his home.

Darkness fell over the town, lights blinking on, yellow candles and oil lamps flickering in the night. Saloons and gambling halls were brightly illuminated by rings hanging from the rafters in which were set hundreds of candles, or by suspended lamps. Music issued from behind batwing doors, and up at the west end a drunken cowboy began shooting off his six-gun and howling his war-cry.

"There goes Happy Jack Morco, one of our marshals, to stop that," Grey explained as a square-set hombre armed with a shotgun rushed past, headed for the gunfire.

Fred Grey was well-off. He had a stable boy who took charge of the horses, although the men preferred to see to their own mounts. Saber had to have a place to himself.

The Rio Kid trailed Bat Masterson to the kitchen stoop. Grey sang out heartily: "Come on in, boys." Vern Burnett, taciturn, seldom speaking save when directly addressed, stalked with long-legged stride at

Pryor's flank, and Celestino trotted at the other. They entered the big kitchen which had a stove for cooking, dish shelves, tables, and was lit by two oil lamps hanging by chains.

A young woman stood there, facing the door. The Rio Kid took her in. She was beautiful, he thought, in her full, long-skirted dress, which had a choker collar. Her face was oval under dark, fine hair, shining with the health of youth. Her lips were full and red. She was trim and neat, with straight nose and level blue eyes. She showed no embarrassment at the arrival of the strangers; rather it was they who became constrained at sight of the pretty girl. Bat Masterson quickly felt of his crimson kerchief, straightened the red sash, took off his fancy hat, whispering to the Rio Kid: "Wisht I'd spruced up 'fore I come in!"

"Gents, meet my daughter, Ruth," Fred Grey said.

Ruth Grey smiled on them all. Vern Burnett stood leaning against the door frame, tall figure tense. He fixed the young woman with his burning, somber eyes. She came to him as she greeted them all individually, and her expression grew sober for a moment. Next she favored the Rio Kid with a word.

"You saved Dad's life." She took his hand. "I'm too grateful to try to thank you."

The Rio Kid smiled. He was overwhelmed by the pretty woman's attention. The softness of her small hand thrilled, and he looked into her eyes.

"Glad to help, Ma'am," he murmured. "But any man'd have done the same. Bat's friends really saved us all."

"Find seats," said Ruth. "I'll see about dinner. I know you're all starved."

Outside were basins and buckets of water, a towel. The men washed up, and then went to sit in a circle in the parlor. Masterson, Pryor, Mireles, Burnett, listened while Fred Grey quickly told them of what had transpired in the past two days.

"Dan Olsen's bin murdered, Ruth tells me, and another dealer, Will Carter, both friends of mine. They were shot at night, and so were a couple of other hombres. Ruth claims that Bull McGlone come around here late, askin' for me. I'll hafta look into it all. We got a sort of association of independent hide dealers in Ellsworth. Sam Wilkins is our head. I'll wanta see Sam."

Savory cooking odors came from the kitchen — coffee and beef, beans and eggs, ham, hot bread, which Ruth Grey quickly

47

shook up for the hungry men. Waiting to eat, they all had a drink. Bob Pryor picked up a rudely printed newspaper, *The Ellsworth Reporter.*

At the top of the first of its four pages black letters blared: "ALL IS QUIET IN ELLSWORTH." This was an attempt to keep the town calm by the power of suggestion, for immediately underneath, the headlines cried: "FOUR HIDE DEALERS MURDERED!" And beside this account: "ED HOGUE, OUR HONEST TOWN MARSHAL, GETS A FREE HAIRCUT FROM MR. CLAY ALLISON OF LAS ANIMAS!"

The haircut mentioned had been executed by carefully placed six-shooter bullets from Mr. Allison's Colt as he stood Ellsworth on its head.

"Say, is Clay in town?" cried Bat Masterson, looking over Bob Pryor's shoulder. "He's okay when he's sober but he's shore hell-bound when he's had a few drinks throwed into him!"

Pryor had heard of Clay Allison, the club-footed Adonis from Las Animas.

Vern Burnett sat, his back straight as a ramrod, on the edge of his chair. He never took his eyes off the doorway through which he could now and then glimpse Miss Grey as she flitted to and fro preparing the meal for the tired and dusty men.

They were just sitting down to the groaning board, piled high with food, when someone knocked on the front door and Ruth Grey went to let the newcomer in. Fred Grey leaped to his feet, shaking hands, escorting the genial visitor to the table.

"Sit and eat with us, Sam," he cried. "Yuh know Bat Masterson — and Vern Burnett. This here young feller's Bob Pryor, better known as the Rio Kid, from Texas way. This lad with him is Celestino Mireles. Boys, this is Sam Wilkins, who heads our hide dealers' association."

Sam Wilkins nodded to them all, let his big, heavy frame down into a chair next Grey. The Rio Kid returned his greeting, looking into the smiling brown eyes. Wilkins had on a dark suit and fine boots, he wore a white shirt and string tie, and the straight black hat he took off exposed his brick-colored, thick hair. His complexion was rather florid and he had a thick-bridged nose and good teeth. All his movements were deliberate, and he seemed an easygoing hombre, good-natured and friendly.

"Your boy come over and gave me yore message, Fred," he remarked.

The Rio Kid pushed the whiskey bottle

toward Wilkins; but the hide dealer shook his head, saying: "No, thanks, don't drink."

Quickly Fred Grey described his narrow escape from death on the plains.

"It was Bull McGlone, Tallifero and Crane, of that I'm shore, Sam. Now why should they be after me thataway?"

Wilkins shook his head, puzzled. "Did you have a quarrel with any of McGlone's bunch?"

"Nope. Never had anything much to do with 'em, though I did buy some hides last season from Crane. How 'bout these other dealers that were shot and kilt the other night?"

"Huh. It's also a puzzle," growled Sam Wilkins, frowning. "Olsen's widder claims Bull McGlone was there. Bull admits it, but says somebuddy shot Olsen through the winder, from the porch, and he didn't see who it was."

"Purty thin," Grey remarked.

The Rio Kid listened to the sharp talk of the hide dealers. His eyes, however, were busy watching Miss Ruth's goings and comings as she tended the table.

"What had we better do, Fred?" asked Wilkins.

"My idea is to arrest McGlone and charge him with attempted murder," Grey said determinedly.

"That'll mean a war," Wilkins declared. "McGlone's got a big followin' of gunmen and tough hunters. Why, there's not a marshal in town with the nerve to take Nebraska Bull!"

"Maybe there ain't now," Grey agreed, "but there soon will be!" His eyes flitted for a moment to the Rio Kid. "There's somethin' shady goin' on in these parts, and McGlone's back of it. We got to find out what it is, Wilkins, and pertect ourselves."

"Reckon you're right," Sam Wilkins said.

A volley of gunshots banged outside. Confused yells and the drumming of a fast-ridden horse came to them over the general howl of Ellsworth. Young Bat Masterson leaped to his feet with such rapidity that he overturned his chair. He hustled to the parlor window, looked out.

"It's Clay Allison," he said, grinning at the Rio Kid. "He's come in ag'in. Let's go see the fun."

Chapter V
New Marshal

Bob Pryor stood in the shadows under the wooden awning, Bat Masterson beside him, Celestino Mireles at his mentor's elbow.

Out in the middle of the plaza a man sat a snow-white horse. His clear, vibrant voice could be heard in the unnatural silence which had come upon the inhabitants of Ellsworth. A thousand of them had ceased play or labor in which they were engaged to watch the man from Las Animas "hurrah" the town.

Clay Allison stood two inches over six feet, but he stood as little as possible, because of his club foot. No man ever dared even glance at his deformity. But on horseback, where he lived except when he would limp into a saloon for a drink, Allison was strikingly handsome, a symphony in black and white.

He weighed in at 180, broad at the shoulders, tapering to slim hips. He was lithe and quick, with slender hands of which he was inordinately vain. Wavy black hair showed under his black hat, high forehead gleaming in the shafts of light from the many open doorways. The boldness of his dark-blue eyes and aquiline nose set off his good-looking, proud countenance. He was an ace shot with a pistol and rifle.

When celebrating, Allison was a dangerous customer to bump into, although he was not an outlaw or gunman for gain. All the frontier towns knew him, Texas and Kansas,

New Mexico. In the town of Canadian, Texas, Clay had done a Lady Godiva ride on his other war horse, a coal-black mustang, shooting and whooping it up along Main Street. He had killed a good many men, but there was always some loophole of legality through which he could slip: either the opponent had drawn first or tried to, or at least advertised his intention of getting Clay.

"Where are the town marshals?" the Rio Kid growled, as Clay Allison set his white horse in motion. Riding full-tilt up and down, Allison hurrahed the town, putting bullets into windows, into the store fronts. Everybody ducked for cover. After shouting a challenge to the northern marshals to come and make a fight, Clay Allison whirled south between the line of buildings and hit it up for the prairie camps.

Bat Masterson laughed uproariously at the scene.

"Let's go wet our whistles, Kid. I don't git to town ev'ry night. Clay didn't hurt anybuddy tonight, outside of a few winders. He's jist full of animal spirits, I reckon."

They went down under the awnings and entered Jake New's big saloon.

"There's Happy Jack Morco," Bat remarked, pointing to a man down the bar, who was calmly drinking a long whiskey. He wore a town marshal's badge. "When Clay's in town, they're usually sorta deaf," he went on. "Morco ain't scairt but there's no sense tanglin' with Allison 'less he actually kills somebuddy."

Right after Masterson, Celestino and the Rio Kid, a tall man entered the saloon, which was filled with cowboys and gamblers. He shouldered a way to Bat and the Kid, slapped the Kid on the back.

"Howdy, Rio Kid — howdy, Bat, howdy, Mex."

In the mirror, before he turned, Bob Pryor recognized his friend Wyatt Earp.

"Hello, Wyatt, yuh old rapscallion," Bat cried joyfully, pumping the tall hombre's hand.

The Rio Kid, too, was glad to see Earp. No braver man rode the frontier than the lanky, tall man with the deep-set frosty blue eyes and tawny, drooping mustache. The Kid had met Wyatt Earp at Red River Crossing one exciting day when he had helped a group of stranded Texans drive a herd to Kansas. They had fought common enemies together and had quickly grown to be friends.

Earp shook his head to the whiskey bottle.

"What's up, Bat?" he asked.

"Oh, we're plannin' a hunt, Wyatt, down in the Panhandle. How 'bout yuh jinin' us?" Masterson asked.

Earp shook his head. "Thanks, Bat. I mean to hunt alone this season."

"Huh?" Bat's mouth dropped open. "Say, yuh'll lose yore hair. 'Sides, yuh won't make any profit."

Earp shrugged. "I figger diff'rent. I'll take wagons and a skinner. I kin kill twenty-five good bulls a day and make a good profit that I'll git to myself after payin' my skinner."

"Yuh won't come to the 'Dobe Walls, then?"

"Nope, not this time. And I'm leavin' my Sharps behind, Bat. I'm usin' a breech-loadin' shotgun instead."

Bat Masterson threw up his hands in despair. All right-minded buffalo hunters used a .50 caliber Sharps, weighing from 16 to 20 pounds, and it was the best weapon for killing buffalo from long range. However, as Wyatt Earp went on to explain, he meant to get in close and make every shot count.

"Yuh know, Kid," Earp said earnestly, "a buffalo'll run like hell soon as he sees or smells a man on hossback. But he won't move when yuh creep up on foot. Yuh take yore stand behind a bush and yuh kin shoot a dozen in a stand 'fore they'll even git it into their dumb heads to start walkin'."

"That's true," agreed Bat.

They spoke of more technical points of their trade. Buffalo hunters, far from riding madly after galloping animals and shooting them from horseback, used stealth. It was as simple as knocking over so many statues, provided the beasts did not, when they finally stampeded, run down the hunter in his stand, or the Indians did not sneak up on the marksman.

An hour later, Mayor Fred Grey, accompanied by Sam Wilkins and two other hide dealers, entered Jake New's. They waved to the Rio Kid, and approached Marshal Happy Jack Morco.

"Evenin', Jack," Grey said gravely. "I got a warrant for the arrest of Nebraska Bull McGlone and I want yuh to fetch him in and lock him up tonight."

Happy Jack nearly choked on the swallow of liquor he had just taken.

"What?" he growled. "Me arrest Bull McGlone? Say, yuh must be loco, Fred."

"Why not?" demanded Grey. "He tried to murder me between Salina and here."

Morco's brown face cleared.

"Oh, well," he replied. "That lets me out, Mayor. I got enough to do in town 'thout policin' the hull damn prairie. Why, Bull McGlone's got a gang of gun-fighters that could wipe out the army! If yuh tried to arrest him, he'd open up and slaughter the town."

"You see," Sam Wilkins said despairingly. "It's no use, Fred. McGlone's too strong for us."

The Rio Kid broke the silence.

"Where's McGlone now?" he said.

"Over in Brennan's saloon. There a big game on, stakes enough to choke a buffalo. Ben and Bill Thompson are sittin' in, and Pete Tallifero, One-Shot Harry Crane and Cad Pierce."

Fred Grey questioned the Rio Kid with his troubled gaze. A half smile showed the Kid's white teeth. In his blue eyes shone the devil-may-care light of a man who has faced death so often that it has become familiar, almost enjoyable.

Grey suddenly reached in his pocket, drew out a town marshal's badge. The assent in Pryor's eyes caused him to raise his hand and pin the star on the Kid's vest flap.

"I appoint yuh special marshal to deal with the disorder in Ellsworth," Fred Grey said sonorously.

Wyatt Earp and Bat Masterson said nothing, but watched the play. Individualists,

they had not been personally attacked by
Bull McGlone and they did not feel justified in interfering in the feud. But when
their pard, the Rio Kid, took on the status
of town marshal, Earp drawled: "We'll drift
along and see fair play."

Bat Masterson grinned in agreement,
drained his glass and hitched up his gun-
belt.

"Go to it, Kid," he cried. "It's yore play.
We'll see yuh ain't drygulched."

Across the dark face of Celestino Mireles
drifted a shadow of alarm. He loved the Rio
Kid, practically worshiped the man who had
snatched him from death in Mexico. The
lad's deep-set eyes burned with anxiety. His
proud head was high as with mingled admi-
ration and worry for Bob Pryor, he trailed
after the procession which started for Brennan's.

The Rio Kid ducked under the hitch-rack
and took to the dusty street paralleling the
K.P. tracks. It was less crowded with surg-
ing humanity than the narrow wooden
sidewalk under the awning. Horses stood in
long lines, awaiting their masters, and,
oblivious to the sudden threat of dramatic
violence that hung over Ellsworth, the
cowboys howled.

Out in front walked the Rio Kid, guns

belted at his slim waist, gait relaxed and easy. A short distance behind came Earp and Masterson, flanking him. Then came Grey and Wilkins. Finally, bringing up the rear, were Happy Jack Morco and Celestino Mireles, the Mexican lad flitting along like a shadow.

"There's Brennan's," called Mayor Fred Grey.

Ahead loomed a large saloon and gambling hall. The Kid noted the hasty hombre who ran inside.

"Reckon McGlone's got spies out," he mused. "He'll be ready for us."

The Rio Kid made a military left turn, ducked under the rail between standing saddle horses, and went up on the stoop. His eyes were ahead. He knew that his friends would protect him from a rear shot any drygulcher might attempt. He stalked through the batwings and paused inside the main room, sweeping it with his eyes.

Sawdust strewed the floor, damp with spilled beer and whiskey. Men lined the bar two and three deep. A piano and violin were playing in one corner, and men sat at tables with painted, gaily frocked girls. At a glance Pryor saw that Bull McGlone was not in the big hall.

He walked straight toward a lighted

double door at the rear, and the chatter of those in the saloon died off as they saw the Rio Kid's lithe figure, caught the glint of light on the metal badge of his office. The grave-faced Fred Grey and Wilkins, Earp and Bat Masterson, and Happy Jack Morco, told them for sure something was up.

The Rio Kid passed one door, first looking through to make sure the earnest gamblers within were not those he sought. At the second chamber he stopped and swung to the room.

At a round table, piled high with cash and chips, sat Nebraska Bull McGlone. The big gunman had on his flat-topped hat. A drinking glass half full of whiskey and a pile of money stood before him. Both his hands showed on the table top, and there was a sneering smile on his thick lips. As he caught the Kid's cold eyes he sniffed, mouth twitching up at the corner.

Ben Thompson and his brother Billy, veteran and professional gamblers, were in the game. Ben scowled at the Rio Kid, whom he had bumped into at Abilene. Billy, being drunk, and hence extremely dangerous and likely to explode any moment, sat next his more famous brother. Pete Tallifero sat tense as did One-Shot Harry Crane, flanking their boss, McGlone. They all had on sidearms, but no one made any move, leaving that to Bull McGlone.

For a long moment the Rio Kid stood in the doorway, watching Nebraska Bull. He took in the ugly giant's ferocious face, the squashed nose, blue jowls, dude's black mustache on the twitching lip, small eyes, red with inward rage at the Kid's intrusion.

The Rio Kid, who knew men from his Army days and from his ensuing adventures on the Border and frontier, would have instantly marked McGlone as an extremely dangerous customer on sight, even had he not had the little tilt with Bull on the plains when he had snatched Grey from death. As for Tallifero and Crane, they, too, were killers and gunmen, but they were followers, and not leaders like Nebraska Bull.

In the hall behind the Kid appeared Bat Masterson, Happy Jack Morco and Wyatt Earp.

Chapter VI
Showdown

McGlone's tremendous physical strength emanated from the bulky, steel-muscled figure. His smoldering eyes, clashing with the Rio Kid's straight look, swore an eternal hatred. Nothing but the death of one or the other, the Kid knew, could settle this silent antagonism.

"C'mon," growled Ben Thompson coldly. "It's yore play, Bull. If yuh smell polecat, too, shet the door."

It was, indeed, McGlone's play. The Rio Kid, guns not yet drawn, hands lax at his slim hips, took a step inside the room.

"Sorry to bust up yore game, gents," he drawled, "but I want McGlone. Bull, yuh're under arrest."

A smile spread over the swarthy Mc-Glone's face.

"Well, well," he said gruffly. "If'n that's a polecat it kin talk, Ben!"

Pryor took another step toward McGlone. Within six paces of the big fellow he stopped, took up his stand. Now he knew that he could kill McGlone, even though the others might get him afterward.

"Never mind the smart talk," the Kid said coldly. "Stand up, McGlone, and unbuckle yore gun-belt."

McGlone cursed him, fluently. He kept his seat but he also kept his hands on the round table.

"Get out of here, yuh fool," he ordered thickly. "Yuh're askin' for a bullet."

"In the back?" the Kid said glibly. He

smiled, now, and the look in his eyes held Bull McGlone.

"What the hell —" exploded Billy Thompson, leaping to his feet. Drunk, Billy had grown impatient at the tension. Ben tried to pull him back but Billy fumbled at his gunbelt.

The Rio Kid never looked away from Bull McGlone. An instantaneous slip and McGlone would make his draw, shoot to kill. Pryor left the others to his friends; this was between McGlone and himself.

Happy Jack Morco slid past, behind Pryor's figure. He flashed a six-shooter, barrel rising. They heard the crack of it, sharp as a breaking stick, on Billy Thompson's befuddled head. Thompson folded up, Colt half out of its holster. Brother Ben, seeing Masterson and Earp in the door, sat quietly; he only said: "I'll get yuh for that, Jack."

Tallifero and Crane dared not make a move without Bull first starting the ball rolling.

"Git up on yore hind legs, McGlone," the Rio Kid ordered again. "This is the last time I tell yuh. I'll take yuh out horizontal if yuh can't walk."

"Why, damn yuh —" snarled McGlone.

He shifted! The Rio Kid saw his wrist muscles tauten and the white blur of the giant's hand. Then the Kid made his draw, so fast that it was breath-taking. According to a Western marshal's code, the law-breaker was allowed to start for his gun before the officer drew, and the Rio Kid, who had been given a quick flash of the trouble brewing in the buffalo market, wanted to make it all fair and square with Bull McGlone. He intended to humiliate the big fellow.

The flash of the Army Colt, coming from its supple, oiled holster, no drag to the leather, flicked in the lamplight. McGlone, fast as he was, had only got the cylinder of his heavy revolver from its holster when he found himself staring into the round muzzle of the Kid's gun. Under the Kid's thumb was the hammer, pulled back by the weapon's weight as it rose.

Nebraska Bull McGlone stared death in the eye. He stopped his draw, and slowly raised his big hands over his flat hat.

The Rio Kid was smiling. There was no tenseness in his lithe body. Tallifero spat an angry curse as he saw McGlone beaten to the draw by the Kid. A shot, the first one of the episode, banged in the room and Pete Tallifero grabbed at his forearm, where a slug from Bat Masterson's six-shooter had just furrowed the flesh.

The tinkle of glass sounded from the Kid's

rear. A shotgun muzzle was thrust through the broken window. Wyatt Earp's long Colt roared, once, twice. McGlone's drygulcher, outside the window, shrieked in death as the tall hombre's slugs took him in the face. The shotgun exploded, wadded load tearing a wide hole in the ceiling.

There were men, friends of Bull McGlone, outside the place, no doubt brought by the tipster who had warned the giant of the Kid's approach.

Bob Pryor took another step toward the giant gunny. He did not again repeat his order. McGlone gulped, then he slowly stood up.

"Cut it out," he roared to his men. "Cut it out. I'll go with the fool."

He unbuckled his gun-belt, let it fall to his great boot toes, and stepped out of the circle of death.

Black rage on his twisted face, sniffing in fury, the big fellow stalked out ahead of the Rio Kid, up the hall and through the main saloon.

Relief flooded Ellsworth. Word that Bull McGlone was to be arrested or such an attempt made, had spread far and wide. McGlone was known to have many shady followers, tough hombres who would fight at the drop of a hat.

Guns holstered, the Rio Kid walked outside, keeping back of his prisoner.

"Yuh know where the town lock-up is, McGlone," he said casually.

McGlone growled at him. Masterson and Earp, the Mayor, and Sam Wilkins, head of the independent hide dealers of the district, came in a bunch after them. Happy Jack Morco, with Billy Thompson shouldered, staggered along at the rear.

Mayor Fred Grey was delighted with the Rio Kid's nerve, with the showdown. He had a key to the lock-up in the new jail and courthouse on the north side of the tracks, two blocks east of Douglas. The Rio Kid unlocked a cell and Bull McGlone stalked in, sat on the hard wooden bench provided as a bed.

"Yuh'll git yore hearin' tomorrer, McGlone," growled Fred Grey.

McGlone spat, sniffed in contempt. "Try to hold me, Grey," he drawled. "Yuh've made a big mistake."

Happy Jack Morco came puffing in, the still unconscious Billy Thompson on his bent back. He let his prisoner slide into a cell, snapped the lock.

"Phew," he gasped, "he's heavy as lead, gents. Say, Ben's sore. He ran to git his pet shotgun. We better bar the doors."

Grey slapped the Rio Kid on the back, grinning.

"Yuh shore got guts, young feller!"

Increasingly, from outside in the plaza, came the sound of gathering men. Loud voices, shots in the air, told of the excitement. Bob Pryor, McGlone off his hands, looked about him. The windows were heavily barred, the door of thick oak slabs. They could stand a siege if necessary in the building.

"Where'd Celestino go to?" he asked.

Mireles had slipped away, evidently before reaching the lock-up. Knowing the slim lad's courage, the Rio Kid guessed that Celestino must have decided to have a look around in the interests of his friend. Mireles was a genius at pumping information from people, and digging out facts that the Rio Kid might want to know.

The Rio Kid stepped to the front door and went out on the porch. A mob was collecting. Many citizens had come just to see the fun, and stayed back out of direct bullet range, watching the antics of Ben Thompson. The squat gambler-desperado, mustache working in his rage at the arrest of his younger brother, was up on a flat wagon, the sort used to bring in buffalo hides, and was haranguing anybody who would listen.

He had run and brought his pet double-barreled shotgun, a fine weapon which Ben loved.

"Is this a free country?" Thompson bellowed, waving his shotgun over his bare head. "Kin a snake like this Rio Kid arrest gentlemen engaged in a friendly game of kyards and git away with it?"

"Give it to 'em, Ben," shouted a big cowman in halfboots, Stetson and leather pants, a supporter of the Thompsons from Texas.

The Kid stood quietly on the veranda, watching the furious Ben Thompson. Billy was adept, when in his cups, at starting fights and Ben usually finished them. Originally from Texas, Ben had killed a man at the early age of thirteen and run away. The cowtowns of Kansas had known him as a professional gambler and gun-fighter. Though not a criminal in the sense that a holdup man or rustler was, Ben Thompson used the six-gun and rifle to uphold his grisly reputation as a killer. The code was strict and known to all: a man who carried guns was, once he drew one or tried to, fair game for his opponent. The homicide was thereby justified and no Western jury would indict the winner of such a duel.

A shadow slid up under the railing, softly hailed the Rio Kid.

"General! Many men ride from the eas'
— zey are frien's of McGlone. Ze othair two
hav' geeve ordaires to rescue McGlone, keel
you."

"Good boy," the Rio Kid whispered without looking down.

His experienced eye took in the situation.
He had McGlone, meant to hold his man.
Fred Grey came to join him. The mayor was
anxious.

"A lot of the cowboys like Ben Thompson. He worries me more'n McGlone's
bunch just now, Kid."

Ben Thompson was cursing and shrieking
imprecations. He shook his shotgun at the
lithe figure of the Rio Kid, standing at ease
on the veranda.

To the east, up Main, Pete Tallifero and
One-Shot Harry Crane were gathering
cronies about them, horsemen who came
from the direction of Nauchville, a couple
of dozen of them, and more arriving. They
were all heavily armed, their faces were hard
and vicious — gunmen and riffraff of the
frontier, fugitives from other states, killers
of their fellowmen.

"I'd better shut Ben Thompson up,"
drawled the Rio Kid. "Then we kin take
keer of McGlone's hombres."

"Wait — don't go over there —" began

Grey, but the Rio Kid was already on his way, long strides taking him straight toward the cursing, reviling figure on the flat wagon.

Breathlessly, the Mayor watched. Bob Pryor walked easily, hands swinging limply at his slim hips, where his Army Colts remained in their supple holsters. He kept his eye on Ben Thompson, who saw him coming and, leveling the shotgun, roared: "Stand back or I'll fire!"

CHAPTER VII
JUSTICE MOCKS

As he walked on, ever closer toward Ben Thompson's deadly shotgun, the Rio Kid could not yet guess the terrible depths of what he had come upon in his visit to Kansas. Nor could Fred Grey plumb the murderous plans of hidden enemies who were fronted by Nebraska Bull McGlone.

"Draw yore gun and make yore play, Rio Kid," bawled Ben Thompson, grinding his teeth behind his straggly mustache.

Brutal as Thompson was, he would not shoot unless his opponent started a draw or had a gun in hand. That would have been to court lynching or trial for actual murder. The Rio Kid was well aware of the Frontier code. He did not draw a pistol but coolly walked to the edge of the cowboys, crowding about Thompson's wagon. A path was quickly opened. Men drew back, not wishing to take a stray bullet. Ben's friends left the opening of the play to him. Thompson would have considered it a deadly insult if any man had shot the Rio Kid for him.

The Rio Kid stared straight into the ferocious eyes of the gambler.

"Git down offa there, Thompson," he drawled. "Take yore popgun and go back to yore game."

His purpose was to start Ben talking, arguing with him, and he succeeded. Silence fell over the crowd around Thompson, as they heard the new marshal's bold order.

"Rio Kid," snarled Ben, "yuh tangled with me in Abilene and I let yuh git away with it. Ellsworth is goin' to be diff'rent. Draw yore gun and make yore fight. I'll see yuh're buried 'fore the kiotes git yuh."

"Don't be a fool," Pryor said, voice loud and penetrating. "What's Bull McGlone to yuh?"

"Nuthin', but my brother is. Let him go, savvy, 'fore I tear yore jail into pieces and yuh with it."

"Yore brother will sleep off his likker, which he don't hold any too well," drawled the Rio Kid. "In the mornin' he'll pay a small fine and be freed. But if yuh start that jail tearin', Thompson, yore brother's liable as not to get hurt under the fall of it. McGlone's nuthin' to yuh, nor is he anything to yore brother Bill. So why court death by fightin' for Bull? Yuh know yore brother had no cause to horn in on my play against McGlone. You haven't either."

Ben Thompson bit at his mustache.

"No man kin say I ain't fair and square, with kyards or guns."

The shotgun muzzle dropped. Thompson, brought to his senses by the Rio Kid's bold play, realized he was pulling Bull McGlone's chestnuts out of the fire. He cleared his throat, and the Rio Kid, sensing the moment, spoke carefully.

"Do like I said, Ben. Go on back and pick up yore kyards."

Thompson turned his head, scowling at the cowmen about him. Eyes were averted. No one cared to look wrong at Ben Thompson or seem to be critical. Suddenly Ben Thompson began to smile; the smile spread to a grin, and finally he laughed.

"Yuh win, Rio Kid," he cried. "But let Billy out in the mornin'."

He leaped down from the wagon, and pushed his way back toward the saloons.

As the Rio Kid turned, a bullet whirled past his ear. He felt the sting of another that ventilated his Stetson crown, the strap holding the wide hat on his chestnut head. He faced toward the east, and saw Pete Tallifero and One-Shot Harry Crane, among the gunnies who had hurriedly been called in after McGlone's arrest. A couple of them had taken shots at him.

Danger threatened, danger to the crowds in the streets of Ellsworth! A pitched battle might mean death to innocent citizens. McGlone's men came galloping in a bunch, full-tilt, reckless riders spurring deep into the ribs of the snorting, flying mustangs. They kept on the railroad side of the street, dust billowing up from flying hoofs.

The Rio Kid moved back like a flitting shadow, and now both his pistols were in hand. The fusillade from the attacking gunnies tore up the dirt where an instant before he had stood. Wyatt Earp, Bat Masterson, Happy Jack Morco and Fred Grey pushed out on the jail porch, calling to the Kid to run in. They had shotguns and pistols. Citizens and others not involved ducked for cover as heavy guns roared. Bullets were hitting the sides of the jail.

The Rio Kid, never hurrying, backed toward the building where his friends were.

His six-guns blared at the criminal riders who were trying to riddle him. Two men fell from their saddles, one kicked and ground under the hoofs of those behind. The gang sped on, riding like Indians, shooting as they moved.

A slug creased the flesh of the Kid's left forearm. His right-hand Colt blazed an answer, and a man let out a shrill yip of pain. From the porch burst gunfire. Earp and Masterson, expert shots, Fred Grey, and Sam Wilkins, shot toward the hard-faced gunnies.

The gang headed on past the line of the courthouse. They did not fancy the accurate guns of the Rio Kid and his friends. Nor did they return. Instead they rode on out of Ellsworth, and a strange quiet fell suddenly upon the town.

Men began peeking from behind hogs-heads filled with water, set at strategic points to guard against fire, and from the windows of saloons, or dark corners where they had ducked as the battle opened.

Wounded arm dripping blood, the Rio Kid stalked back to the jail.

"I reckon they're gone," he murmured, blowing smoke from his hot guns. He shoved fresh cartridges into the emptied cylinders, let the guns slide back into their holsters.

"Whew!" gasped Fred Grey. "Kid, yuh shore backed 'em into their hole and made 'em pull it after 'em tonight! C'mon, drinks're on me, boys. That was dryin' work."

It was late and the Rio Kid was weary, from the fighting strain and the showdown during his first hours as frontier marshal of Ellsworth. After a round of drinks, he returned to the courthouse, where blankets spread on the floor gave him a bed. Celestino Mireles, after making sure his friend was not seriously hurt, slipped out into the town again. An excellent getter of information, the Mexican youth meant to listen and watch, for signs of danger to his partner, his "general."

Though the Rio Kid did not guess the fact, he had just scratched the surface of the trouble in Kansas.

Vern Burnett sat, stiffly, silently, on the edge of the plush chair in Mayor Fred Grey's parlor. He kept his somber eyes upon Miss Ruth Grey, except at the times when she looked straight at him and smiled. Then he would drop his gaze, afraid she might think him overbold.

She talked to him, trying to draw him out, but he was ill at ease in feminine society. Yet the magnetism of youth held him where he was. A happiness he had never experienced before had come to Vern Burnett.

When Vern Burnett was four years old, his father and mother had started across Kansas in a covered wagon, California bound. The Cheyennes had struck; left the wagon a flaming, horrible funeral pyre, but they had carried the little boy off with them. During the next three years he had lived among the Indians, in a tepee, following the buffalo.

Then had come one of the periodical treaties with the savages, one stipulation of which had been the release of all white prisoners. An army commissioner, backed by troops, had found Vern Burnett, who was practically a young Indian, recognized him as a white, taken him back to frontier civilization. He had an Indian name by that time. Only a small gold locket, which had been hung about the child's neck and had been looked upon by the Indians as a charm, had made identification of the boy possible. It contained a lock of his mother's hair, and the name "Vern Burnett" — that had been his family name and he had accepted it as his.

For four years the little fellow had been watched over by kind soldier women about the forts. At the age of twelve, Vern Burnett had graduated in a day from boyhood to manhood. Like all youths of the Frontier, he had started a man's work early. Tall and large for his age, he had become a teamster, and after a few years, had taken to buffalo hunting.

He had never come in close contact before with a girl like Ruth Grey.

"I've been terribly worried about Father," Ruth told the tall young hunter. "You see, Bull McGlone came here looking for him the other night, and the very next day, they tried to kill him on his way home from Salina. Something's going on, something shady. The very night four other hide merchants were shot. There's no proof against McGlone and his bunch, but it's all very suspicious."

"Yes'm," murmured Burnett. He wanted to say that he would be happy to champion her, and that he would hang Bull McGlone's hide to a fence if necessary. He watched the play of her vivacious features as she talked.

"McGlone's working up some sort of buffalo hide syndicate, they say," she continued. "I think that must have something to do with it, don't you? The syndicate's offering higher prices, six dollars a hide, and promising the hunters all sorts of things. It will put Dad out of business, I'm afraid, and a lot of other independent dealers."

A fusillade of gunshots smashed the night air, and Ruth Grey gave a quick cry, hurried to the window and looked out. Vern Burnett rose, tall figure towering over the girl. He opened the front door and stepped out on the veranda. He saw the whirling horsemen as they passed the courthouse, the Rio Kid and his friends at the jail.

"Reckon I better go over, Ma'am," he told her softly. He drew his six-shooter, and, tall buckskin-clad figure moving with the lithe speed of an Indian brave, started across the plaza.

But his help was not needed. Presently Fred Grey, taking leave of the Rio Kid and Wilkins, went back to his house, Vern Burnett at his side.

"I'll be glad to bring yuh my kill of buffalo, Grey," Vern told the mayor. "And whatever yuh pay will be okay with me."

"Thanks, Burnett, thanks. McGlone's tryin' to hog the bus'ness, I guess, I mean to look into this killin' of hide merchants that took place. It's mighty suspicious, seems to me. Now, if yuh're lookin' for a place to bed down, yuh kin stay with me, Burnett. Plenty of room."

But a house cramped Vern Burnett's style; he could not sleep on a mattress. He thanked Grey, and went out to the barn, where he put his head on a saddle wrapped in his blanket and slept.

He woke with a start after a couple of hours. Instantly his keen animal senses were alert, he knew that there were intruders close. Nostrils wide, eyes piercing the dark shadows about Grey's home, which was silent and without lights, he caught the difference in color as the black shape of a man showed against the brick foundation.

"Huh, now who's that?" he thought. He had his pistol in hand, having reached for it instinctively as he woke. He began to stalk the stalker.

Burnett could move with the soundlessness of an Indian.

Boots off, buckskin clinging soft and silent about his stalwart figure, he crept from shadow to shadow toward the house wall. Then he saw four more men appear from around the building, joining the first.

The wind, coming to him, brought him a smell he at once recognized as kerosene. The soft sloshing of liquid sounded above the faint murmur of the marauders' whispers. Vern Burnett realized what they were up to. One of them struck a match. Dark face masked to the eyes under the broad Stetson, the hombre was touching the flame to the oil poured against the side of Grey's house.

"Set yoreselves, we'll shoot him down when he comes out," Burnett heard.

Burnett triggered. The arsonist fell dead by the blaze which was already licking up the dry wooden upper wall. The explosion of Vern Burnett's big pistol shocked the rest to sudden flight. They paused at the corner to shoot back but he was down low, had shifted his position, and their bullets only rapped dully into the ground. His answering slugs cut splinters from the corner of the house, and they ducked again, running for their horses near at hand.

Vern Burnett leaped to his feet, ran back to seize a horse blanket. He dashed to the fire, and began beating at it with the blanket. He caught it in the nick of time, before it was well started, or nothing could have saved Grey's home. At Vern's feet as he slapped the flames, smothering them with well-placed blows, lay the dead gunny he had downed. Vern's bullet had hit him in the head, instantly killing him.

Fred Grey came hustling out, and Burnett sang out to him. Together they finished off the blaze. Then the Mayor struck a light and they looked over the vicious-faced rat who had set the fire.

"Dunno him," Grey growled, "but I reckon Bull McGlone does. He's bringin' in killers, no doubt of it. Yuh saved us all, Burnett, and I'm shore obliged."

The place quieted down again. Vern Burnett did not sleep much more that night. Dawn broke and he was up with it. Ruth Grey, grateful to him for what he had done, thanked him earnestly as she gave him a hearty breakfast.

About ten o'clock, they went to the courthouse for the trial of Nebraska Bull Mc-Glone. They met the Rio Kid, spruce as though just out of a bandbox. The Kid, formerly an officer in the Union Army, knew how to talk to women, and he was gallant with Miss Grey, too gallant, Vern Burnett thought enviously, wishing he could handle himself with the devil-may-care aptitude of Captain Robert Pryor, better known as the Rio Kid.

The courtroom was crowded. Pete Tallifero, One-Shot Harry Crane, and a dozen more of McGlone's supporters were present; also many spectators, among them Ben Thompson. The judge came in, and took his seat.

The Rio Kid, as town marshal, had a special seat up front. He watched the magistrate as the latter, with great dignity, took a small flask of whiskey from his back pocket, had a drink, and rapped for order.

The judge was a dandy in dress. He wore a black-and-white checked suit, a flowing silk necktie and starched, pleated white shirt. His boots were of the softest, finest calfskin. His face was sharp, sharp as a weasel's. His eyes, under frowning, thick brows, were glintingly observant and had the same sharpness. Not yet of middle age, he had a bald spot in the crown of his black hair, which was touched gray at the temples. He licked the whiskey off his thin lips, cleared his throat and cried: "Bring in the fust case."

Billy Thompson, grinning sheepishly, for he was now sober, was piloted in by Happy Jack Morco, and stood up before the bar of justice.

"What's the charge?" the judge demanded impatiently, frowning over his glasses.

"Drunk and disorderly, yer honor, Jedge Lask."

Judge Newbold Lask stared sourly at Billy Thompson.

"This is the fourth time you've been here this month, Thompson. Fifty dollars fine. Next time it'll be a hundred."

Ben Thompson came strutting up, planked down the fine, and remarked: "Don't spend it all on drink, Jedge."

"That'll cost you twenty-five dollars more, contempt of court," Lask said icily.

Ben grinned at the Rio Kid, put down the money, and swaggered out arm in arm with his brother.

The Rio Kid, Burnett noticed, had his eyes on the judge.

"Now what's worryin' him, I wonder?" mused Vern.

He took a closer look at the magistrate. Yes, maybe the Kid was right. "He's a crook, a hundred to one," Burnett decided.

Morco fetched in Bull McGlone, and Vern Burnett, who was a close observer of humanity and a judge of men himself, saw the different shine of Judge Lask's eyes.

This was the important case. Mayor Fred Grey went up, and other witnesses.

"Attempted murder, yore honor," Grey told the bench gravely. "He ought to be held for jury trial. This feller, Bull McGlone, and some of his men, tried to kill me."

"That's the truth, Jedge," drawled the Rio Kid.

Lask, corners of his thin-lipped mouth sourly depressed, listened to the evidence. Then he turned to McGlone, who was sniffing in contempt, dog-eyeing the Kid and Grey.

"What's your side of the story, McGlone?" Lask inquired.

"Why, Jedge," Bull replied easily, "there's nothin' to it at all. It's true me 'n some of the boys had a little sport with Grey. We was full of likker and just shot in the air some to skeer him."

Tallifero and One-Shot Harry Crane corroborated the giant's lie. There were others present who swore that no harm had been meant.

Lask raised his hand, frowning on Grey and Pryor.

"This is silly," he growled. "You have no basis for your charge. McGlone, you're fined twenty-five dollars for disorderly conduct. Get out."

Vern Burnett saw the blood flush the face of the Rio Kid.

"He's shore sore! It's plain that jedge has bin bought, he's lettin' McGlone go free! Why, that ain't justice!"

Triumphantly Bull McGlone threw down the small fine, and strode from the courthouse, trailed by a dozen of his pals. Fred Grey was stunned, but as last found his voice.

"Now look, Lask, you've no right to let McGlone go free! He's a murderin' gunman and he's behind them other killin's, I tell yuh —"

"Shut up, Grey," snapped the judge, rising quickly. He reached in his pocket, drew forth his flask, threw back his head and drank. With a scowl at the mayor and the Rio Kid, he left the room.

Vern Burnett edged toward Grey who was talking earnestly with Bob Pryor. Sam Wilkins came over to join them.

"I was afraid of that, Fred," Wilkins growled. "Lask's a friend of McGlone's."

"Yeah, they bought him off," Grey declared angrily.

As for Bob Pryor, he had regained his usual carefree manner.

"Reckon there's not much to be done, Grey," he said easily. He unpinned the marshal's star from his vest and tendered it to the Mayor. "That sorta lets me out."

Anger burned Vern Burnett, though his long, stern face showed no sign of emotion. He had not been brought up among red men without acquiring some of their traits, one of which was to hide what was felt inside. He was angry at the lithe Rio Kid, believing that Pryor had allowed himself to be bluffed by Bull McGlone and his criminal "Syndicate."

"I reckon," drawled the young buffalo hunter, unveiling his long-lashed brown eyes to meet the agate blue stare of the Rio Kid, "that some places are too tough for some folks."

Chapter VIII
Frontier Marshal

Pryor faced the tall hunter. There was a deep vertical wrinkle between his eyes. He was boiling inwardly and Burnett's ill-timed remark topped his aggravation. After risking his life to arrest Bull McGlone, he had seen Judge Lask, the Law in Ellsworth, turn the big man loose with a picayune fine and a reprimand to those who had brought him in and charged him. From this the Rio Kid could guess what came next and from there on: no matter how many men he fetched in, the court would turn them loose.

In the future Bull McGlone and his merrymen, so long as they were a trifle careful about their killings, could get away with anything and no enemy of the Syndicate would be safe in Ellsworth. Fred Grey had been elected mayor, but the Rio Kid knew only too well the inertia and apathy of the townsfolk who could be swayed by a few clever brains. He was aware that, the Law leaning over to aid Bull McGlone, would probably fall on anybody who sought to squeeze between. Those who killed any of McGlone's favorites would be liable to prosecution just as crooked as McGlone's defense had been.

And now Vern Burnett had to stick in his oar work: "Some places are too tough for some folks!"

"Some places," glibly paraphrased the Rio Kid, his tongue sharp and quick from his training as an army officer, "are so full of rattlesnakes that decent folks stay away."

"Meanin' what?" growled Burnett, stepping toward him.

Both were angry, and violent antagonism flared. There was, between these two vigorous young frontiersmen, a hidden reason for antagonism. That reason now stepped between them in person — Ruth Grey.

"Oh, please," she cried, "please! Vern, you shouldn't have said that. The Rio Kid's right in his way, you know. Besides, we can't talk here. Let's go over to the house."

Bob Pryor walked silently, on one side of the pretty girl, Vern Burnett, looking straight ahead, on the other. Mayor Grey and Bat Masterson, Wyatt Earp and Sam Wilkins came in a bunch, talking over the court's action. Bull McGlone stood across the plaza, by a saddled horse. Tallifero and

Harry Crane were talking to a couple of buffalo hunters on a nearby corner.

Wyatt Earp stopped at the stoop of Grey's home. He shook hands all around.

"I'm due to pull out inside of an hour, gents," he drawled.

"Yuh better change yore mind, Wyatt, and come to the 'Dobe Walls with us," cried young Bat Masterson. "We got the Indians scairt of us, in the Panhandle. The 'Dobe Walls makes a right handy headquarters. Hanrahan's even got a saloon there, and yuh kin buy yore supplies without freightin' 'em through."

Wyatt Earp shook his head. "I'm huntin' alone," he insisted. He nodded to the Rio Kid. "Good luck, Pryor. It's none of my bus'ness but any town that figgers a marshal's life at twenty-five dollars *is* one of them snake holes yuh mention."

Earp's plans were made. These frontiersmen were individualists. If the Rio Kid needed help while Earp was around, the tall jigger would give it, to the death. But life had to go on. Danger was so commonplace to these fellows that threats were nothing.

So Wyatt Earp, with his Mexican skinner and flat wagons, pulled out of Ellsworth forty minutes later, bound for the buffalo range southwest of town.

Inside Fred Grey's parlor, the Rio Kid, his first heated rage passing, began to smile. Reckless and devil-may-care, the humorous side of the affair struck him and he laughed. Ruth Grey glanced questioningly at him. She guessed what he was thinking, and smiled gaily with him. Burnett still scowled.

Grey hooked his thumbs in his sagging cartridge belt, faced the gathering. He addressed the Rio Kid. In his hand he still held the marshal's star he had pinned on Pryor and which the Kid had returned at the courthouse.

Sam Wilkins listened, face serious. There were Burnett, Bat Masterson, Ruth and her father, the Kid. Celestino Mireles was not around. He was, the Kid mused, probably hobnobbing with the Mexicans of Ellsworth. In the shanties and sod houses of the lowly, much information could be gleaned.

"Now look, Pryor," Grey began, "I was elected mayor last fall by the folks here. Most of 'em are decent people. They don't tote guns and they like law and order. 'Course there's allus men like McGlone and his bunch, and the town is purty wild, and with the Texas men comin' up the trail and the hunters and all. They like their fun and like it rough. What we need right now is a marshal who's tougher'n the hull passel of 'em and from what I've seen, yuh're it."

The compliments fell off the Rio Kid's shoulders like water off a duck's back.

"I handed back that badge, Grey," he said slowly, "not because I'm afraid of McGlone and his gang, but because I won't buck the Law. It looks to me as though yuh're holdin' a second-best hand in Ellsworth. Yuh kin appoint marshals but the courts undo their work. That's all. If I run into Bull McGlone and he winks wrong, why, that will be different. But he's too foxy to give me a good excuse to shoot him."

"Isn't it plain," Ruth said softly, "that Lask was fixed to let McGlone go?"

"Plain as day," agreed Pryor. "In other words, there's somebody more than McGlone in this. There's citizens who have enough power to buy a jedge and override the police and Grey."

"Why say that?" asked Wilkins.

"Because McGlone ain't the stamp of sidewinder who fights behind a screen," the Rio Kid answered keenly. "McGlone's a gunman, and he believes in force."

"Then," Ruth cried eagerly, "we must find who's back of McGlone and the Syndicate. Will you stay and do it, Rio Kid — Bob?"

The Rio Kid hesitated. He had been drawn into this fight by his meeting with

Grey and his willingness to assist a man in trouble. Now he found that he was becoming involved in a deep affair whose end was not in sight, and in which much blood must stain the prairie earth before the end.

Ruth's level blue eyes appealed to the Rio Kid. In his restless journeyings from the Border to Kansas, Bob Pryor had seen many women, but he had never met one who coupled such beauty with a clever mind.

"I know and Dad knows," Ruth Grey said earnestly, "that you're not afraid of Bull McGlone. But you're our last hope, Bob. If you won't help us, nobody can. I feel that. Please take back the marshal's star and make Ellsworth safe for decent folks."

The Rio Kid bit his lips. He sensed that ahead lay a hard and thankless road.

"Okay," he drawled. "Pin it on me, Miss Ruth."

With a glad cry, she fastened the badge to his vest lapel, and he looked into her pretty eyes, at the flushed, pink cheeks.

Vern Burnett rose. "I'll be goin'," he muttered.

But she seized his hand. "You've got to help us, too, Vern. Please, shake hands with Bob."

The Rio Kid's anger had passed; he smiled

at Burnett's solemn countenance.

"No hard feelin's, Burnett. We need friends."

Vern shrugged. "I'm with yuh," he declared. It took a hard fight for the buffalo hunter to overcome the jealousy within, but he was beginning to realize what it was and was ashamed.

"First thing to do, Grey," the Rio Kid began, "is for yuh to speak to all yore hide-dealer pals. It's plain this McGlone Syndicate's set on wipin' 'em out or buyin' 'em over. Yuh want to band together more solid and it'll be one for all and all for one, savvy? Perfect each other. Yuh'll hafta meet the Syndicate's price per hide, too."

Fred Grey shook his head sadly.

"We can't pay six dollars apiece and last, Kid. It would bust us in no time at all. I don't see how this here Syndicate kin do it."

The Rio Kid thought it over.

"Must be a catch to it, I'll have to find out 'bout that. First, warn yore friends to be careful whom they open their doors to at night and watch their steps after dark. Don't give McGlone any chance, the way Olsen and Carter did. In the meantime, I'll see what I can see, Burnett, I s'pose yuh'll sell yore hides to Grey or the independent dealers, and keep clear of this Syndicate?"

"That's understood," Burnett replied.

"Bat, how 'bout yuh? Yore friends are well known and what they do will have a lot of effect on other hunters. Can you keep 'em in line for Grey?"

Bat Masterson shrugged.

"I'll see what I kin do, Rio Kid. 'Course, profit's profit. The boys ain't in this just for the sport of havin' their hair lifted by the Indians." The handsome Masterson rose, started for the door. "I'll see what I kin do," he repeated.

"I'll go with yuh," the Kid said. "Grey, yuh better start organizin' a tight bunch among yore friends." He nodded and went out the front way with Bat Masterson.

They found Jim Hanrahan in Jake New's saloon. Hanrahan, who had a big stake in Adobe Walls, the far-off, isolated buffalo camp on the Canadian River where it flowed through the northern part of the Texas Panhandle, was a quiet-spoken, big plainsman. He had a great deal of influence among the buffalo hunters, who used his saloon at Adobe Walls as range headquarters.

"I jist signed up with Bull McGlone's Syndicate, Bat," Hanrahan drawled in reply to Masterson's question. "They're guaranteein' six dollars each for hides, good or bad. Billy Dixon and the others have all gone with this here Syndicate. Dunno how long it'll last, that price is too high for 'em to profit. Harry Crane's an old hand at huntin' buffalo, he's in with 'em. They'll either guarantee yuh six dollars a hide or else pay yuh two hundred dollars a month to hunt for 'em, furnish yore lead and grub on the job."

"How many's McGlone got signed up, yuh reckon?" asked Bob Pryor.

"Most ev'rybuddy, I hear. It's the best price ever offered. It'll put independent dealers outa the game, shore enough."

"And then," drawled the Rio Kid, "the Syndicate'll pay yuh two dollars or fifty cents or anything they fancy, Jim."

Hanrahan shrugged, gulped down his whiskey.

"By that time," he remarked, "we'll all be ridin' in private cars, Kid, rich as Croesus at six a skin!"

Chapter IX
In the Devil's Den

Ellsworth began waking up in the late afternoon. Cowboys rode in from outlying camps, readying up for the night of sport.

Freighters, soldiers on leave, gamblers, buffalo hunters, appeared in the light of the sinking sun. Ellsworth was getting prepared to howl.

The Rio Kid, having consented to retain his post of town marshal, took some necessary precautions. Bull McGlone and his cronies had disappeared, ridden east toward Nauchville earlier in the day. But the Kid purchased or borrowed several double-barreled shotguns, loaded them, and left them around at strategic points. He had one behind the bar at Jake New's Saloon, another inside the Grand Central Hotel. He placed a shotgun wherever he figured he might need one quickly and could get his hands on it. It was the recognized weapon for cowing a mob.

In his belt rode two Army Colt .45s. Underneath his shirt were concealed another pair of revolvers. When dark fell and the new marshal took up his patrol to maintain law and order in Ellsworth, he knew just where to lay his hands on his armaments, and had investigated the back ways and Tin Can Alley.

"Wonder where Celestino's keepin' hisself," he mused.

The Mexican lad had been gone all day,

and he did not appear even at meal time.

The evening was quiet, so far as any police work went. The Rio Kid, badge pinned to his vest, guns in holsters, strolled the main street, keeping order. He took a six-shooter away from a drunken cowboy and broke up a fight starting between a couple of soldiers and two buffalo hunters, forcing them all to check their guns.

Always wary, on his toes, expecting trouble from Bull McGlone, yet there was no sign from the enemy. Mayor Fred Grey came to him, informed him that during the afternoon he had spoken to a dozen independent hide dealers who had all agreed to stick together for protection.

"We're behind yuh, Pryor," Grey said earnestly, "and we'll back yuh up."

It was close to midnight when the Kid, turning at the west end to stroll back along the line of lighted buildings, suddenly whirled, and his six-gun emerged from its holster with the speed of a sunbeam.

"Queeck draw, General!" a familiar voice whispered — it was the faint footstep in the inky black alleyway which had caused the Rio Kid to swing.

The Kid shoved his iron back into its leather case. He slid to the narrow, black opening between two storehouses.

"Celestino! Where yuh bin all day?"

Now, closer in, he caught the gleam of the youth's dark and shining eyes, could make out the thin figure.

"I go where I hear what ees really so, General," Mireles told him, voice down low. "Eastward ees where the lowly live. There I fin' those who savvy what goes on!"

"What did yuh find in Nauchville?" demanded Pryor.

"Zat Bull McGlone ees ver-ee strong, General. He has more men zan before, a hundred here, zey say. Gunmen, queeck to shoot. Firs', zey mean to keel you, General. You spoil McGlone's game, so I hear McGlone say."

"Yuh *heard* him?"

"*Si.* Zey meet in saloon, 'Blue Boffalo' she ees call'. A *muchacho,* of my race and age, he sweep' out and wait on table. *Si,* and he hav' loft, above zis back room where McGlone loves to go. You come, General? McGlone ees zere now, weeth othairs."

"Shore I'll come. Wait'll I saddle up. Where's yore hoss?"

"Behind me, General. Peek me up here."

The Kid hustled down the shaded wooden sidewalk. He met Happy Jack Morco across from Grey's and spoke to him.

"I'll be back in an hour or two, Jack. Keep

an eye on things."

"Okay," Morco growled. "I on'y hope it won't git shot out. But things are quiet tonight."

Ten minutes later the Rio Kid was in his saddle on Saber's back. The dun, black stripe shivering on his mousey hide, was glad to see his master. The Kid softly whistled "Said the Big Black Charger," and the fighting, bony dun rolled his eyes, one brown like most horses, the other mirled with marble-blue streaks.

Celestino picked him up as he came galloping to the alley, and they rode east, parallel with the tracks, skirting water tanks, and cow corrals, keeping north of the railroad.

Celestino, the Kid learned, had all day been making friends with Pancho Gasca, a Mexican boy who was sweeper, waiter and spittoon-cleaner of the Blue Buffalo in Nauchville.

"Pancho, he ees beesy now," Celestino said, "but I hav' permeesion to use hees room. Zere is back way up, at one side — and no window zere, for McGlone to see out."

Nauchville gave off an evil, red glow. Smoke hung over the crowded, ill-made buildings, bunched like chicken coops. Sod and odds-and-ends of lumber had been thrown together here; some were only tents, with built-up earth sides. The dives were so low, their business so shady, that even Ellsworth would not allow them within a mile of town.

Sour music and the hum of voices was audible. The Rio Kid, aware of Mireles' ability as a spy, followed the Mexican youth's orders. He dismounted, took off his Stetson and spurs, and left Saber hidden in the darkness of scrawny bush above Nauchville, picketed near Celestino's mustang. Then, the two of them, moving with the speed and stealth of shadows, started for the back of the Blue Buffalo.

There was an oil lamp lit in a rear room of the place. The shaft of light from the window touched the black entryway of the closed door; and as the Rio Kid, getting down low as Mireles did, stared in, he saw the shape of a man's Stetson against the faint illumination outside.

"A guard," he thought.

Foot by foot, using as cover a low fence and piles of rusting tin cans that had been flung from the back doors of the crowded shacks, Mireles led the Kid past the line of the sentry, and started up a narrow, ladder-like outside staircase.

It was pitchblack there and the Kid had

to feel his way. At the top, Mireles touched his hand in caution. The little board door opened, inch by inch. Mireles disappeared inside, but he reached forth to guide the Rio Kid.

"Stay down, put your head to floor, General," he breathed. "Quiet —"

The Rio Kid didn't need to be cautioned. The floor was of loose boards laid on flimsy rafters, and the slightest slip might warn those below.

Heavy voices drifted up, rising and falling in gruff volume. The tiny loft under the eaves smelt of musty clothes and stale tobacco smoke which had come through cracks in the board floor, forming the ceiling below. Now the Rio Kid, eyes growing focused to the darkness, could trace those cracks by faint streamers of yellow light fogged by the smoke.

Music came from the main saloon in front, a tinny piano, and this general noise drowned any slight creakings the two might make as they lowered themselves flat and lay there, listening.

"Have another slug, Harry." That was Bull McGlone, inviting his pard to a drink.

"Okay, Bull," growled One-Shot Harry Crane.

There were at least half a dozen men

below. Pete Tallifero spoke up, voice thick with liquor.

"Why not lemme git that polecat marshal, Bull? I kin do it from that empty store next New's saloon. I kin set in there with a rifle and some of our boys kin shoot off their guns. The fool'll come chargin' out and I'll have him."

"Yuh're goin' to have yore chanct, Pete," McGlone agreed, "and pronto. But this Rio Kid hombre's stumped, it makes me laugh to watch him. He's bilin' inside but he savvies that if he arrests us, the jedge is our friend and'll turn us loose. He can't make up his mind what to do next. The Chief says we'll kill Pryor in a day or two but to let the town calm down a bit. We've signed up a lot of hunters, promised 'em ev'rything in sight."

Tallifero laughed. "Promises are cheap, Bull. They fell for it all. Wait till they fetch in their hides and take what we give em."

"Mebbe trouble, when they find they're beat," growled Crane. "Some of 'em, Jim Hanrahan and Masterson, are tough fellers."

"Say," McGlone cried, "I'll have two hunderd guns on 'em by the time they pull back here with their season's kill. There won't be no other dealers by that time, in Ellsworth, Dodge or Wichita. They'll sell to the Syndi-

cate or let their hides rot. Chief's got it figgered to a T and I'm right with him.

"Harry, the hunters are up to you. Yuh
know their ways and yuh kin lead 'em by
the nose. Pete and me'll handle the fightin'
men we brought in. We'll own Kansas. We
already got thirty thousand hides we took
offa them lousy dealers, and we'll control
the hull market soon. Grey's the main
trouble, but soon as Masterson and his
bunch pull out for the 'Dobe Walls, we'll git
him and the Rio Kid too. Earp left today,
he's gone alone. We'll handle other dealers
like we did Carter and Olsen."

"How 'bout this pertective business
they're gittin' up?"

"That'll fall to pieces when Grey and this
skunk Rio Kid are in Boot Hill." McGlone
cursed hotly, with a sulphurous hatred as he
mentioned Bob Pryor. "He thinks he backed
me down. I'll show him who's tough in
these parts. Hey, yuh Pancho, fetch another
bottle."

McGlone pounded on the table for the
Mexican lad who waited on the back room,
then resumed his instructions.

"See here, Durham, I got yuh up from the
Pecos 'cause yuh ain't known in these parts.
Yuh kin run yore men in and work quiet.
There's a dealer named Moore, Phil Moore,

has 'bout fifteen thousand new hides in his yards. He lives in a shack right by it, yuh know where it is on Main Street?"

"Yeah, I seen it, Crane pointed her out," a deep voice replied.

"Moore's next on the program," continued McGlone. We'll git him tomorrer night. Here's how yuh work it. Yuh ketch him alone, late. Yuh force him to sign over his hides. Then — yuh know what to do next."

"And s'pose this here Marshal Pryor shows up while I'm busy with Moore?"

"We'll take keer of the Rio Kid," McGlone promised. "We'll let Tallifero work his little trick at the same time yuh're arguyin' with Moore. We mean to make our headquarters at Moore's big yard —"

A sudden silence fell upon the gathering below. The Rio Kid, alert and ready, raised his head. He felt Mireles' thin hand touch his wrist.

"Huh?" Bull McGlone demanded. Then: "What the hell's —" But the giant hombre broke off.

"Sounds as though someone come to the door, signalled him a warnin' —"

Bob Pryor rose up, a Colt .45 in his hand. Celestino was right with him, his favorite weapon, a 12-inch bladed knife with a staghorn handle, glinting in his bony grip.

The Rio Kid peeked from the door. The stairs looked clear but it was inky black below. The rickety building shook with the moving tread of heavy men in the room where Bull McGlone had been. As the Kid, the scarred flesh over the old wound in his ribs twitching him a danger signal, stepped out on the platform, he saw the darker blob of the sentry move at the corner of the building.

"Hey, yuh —"

"Down, Celestino," hissed the Kid, ducking. The revolver in the guard's paw flashed blue-red death. Through the Rio Kid's dropping Stetson the bullet tore a hole, zipping on into the night.

Like an echo, the Rio Kid's Colt snapped an answer, and the flame stabbed straight at the dark thickness of the man, shown up by the flaring of his own shot.

The Kid, Celestino on his heels, went leaping down the steps, groaning under their weight. The back door opened. Bunched, armed men, blinded by the lights inside, started forth, cutting them off from the direct path to their horses.

Chapter X
Gun-fight

Who the hell's that?" roared Bull McGlone, behind his pards.

The Rio Kid fired once into the hombres in the door, for their guns were up as they started out to intercept the vague, shadowy forms flitting up the alleyway. He glimpsed, through the gang of gunnies, a dandified figure in a white-and-black checked suit, a ruffled shirt and string tie, the angry, red face of a man he had met in Ellsworth — Judge Newbold Lask.

Bob Pryor's bullet ripped through a man's forearm and plugged with a dull thump into the side of the door. The wounded one screeched, backed up, spoiling the concerted volley that hunted for the Rio Kid and Celestino Mireles. They heard the whoosh of heavy .45 slugs, too high to touch them.

"Fetch yore boys, Durham!" McGlone bawled. "Pronto, now. They're outside there — don't let 'em git free!"

The Rio Kid ran, shoving Mireles before him, up the side alley. He ducked across to another path between houses. People were out in the dusty, crooked street. The Rio Kid and the Mexican youth slowed, weapons out of sight, proceeded as though just two more spectators. Girls in short-skirted red-and-blue spangled dresses peered anxiously from murky windows of dives. Drunken men lurched through the batwings. The hubbub at the Blue Buffalo was still loud, and fierce-faced gunnies, called by Pecos Durham, were running to the spot.

"There he goes," a guttural voice shouted. "It's the Rio Kid!"

Someone on the rickety wooden sidewalk had spied the Kid's lithe figure as he turned into an alley off the lighted way. A bullet cut the corner behind them. A fusillade began, Colts popping, shotguns roaring, and gunnies ran toward them.

Nauchville teemed with their enemies. The two, forced to detour from the direct line to the horses, ran full-tilt for the back yards again. He paused, looked over low fences to the back door of the Blue Buffalo. There were more gunnies, spreading out.

It was useless to try to hide now. Alert and on the prowl, McGlone's killers were rapidly forming a circle to hem them in.

They ran toward the horses, behind the shadows of the low fence.

Innate caution, his experience as a scout for General George A. Custer in enemy country, was all that saved the Rio Kid at that moment from running into certain death. He stopped so suddenly that his heels dug up dirt, and Celestino bumped into him.

"Look out — they're at the hosses," breathed the Rio Kid.

He whistled shrill bars, "Said the Big Black Charger," Saber's favorite tune, the old army call. The dun with the black stripe down his spine instantly responded — he reared high, his sharp forehoofs coming down on the skull of the man who had laid hold of his reins. There was the hollow sound, like a large eggshell cracking — a scream, that died off to a groan and ended in a death gurgle.

Vague shadows leaped erect, Colts blasting bullets at the Rio Kid and Mireles, crouched down. The Kid felt the sting of one that bit the flesh of his forearm, another nipped his left ear. There were several hombres who had been lying in wait for them, at the spot where they had left their horses.

"Fight, Saber," shouted the Kid.

Saber acted like a mad thing. Rearing, snorting, hoofs flying out, biting viciously, the dun spread havoc among the four remaining gunnies. One rolled over and over, arm cracked by the impact of a heavy, hard hoof; another was bowled to earth by the weight of the dun striking him.

The Rio Kid fired, skilfully, carefully, not wishing to harm his pet. He got one of the black, shadowy figures, sent him reeling back. The other one started to run, firing as he went. It was Celestino, white teeth gleaming in the starlight, whose keen knife, thrown at a distance of twelve paces, put him out of the fray.

"C'mon, no time to lose," called Pryor, for Celestino had paused, was kneeling over his victim. The knife blade had driven deep between the hombre's shoulders.

"My bes' knife, General," Celestino said quietly, as he leaped to the Kid's side.

Saber was up, nuzzling his master's hand. The Kid hit leather without touching iron. Mireles' horse was starting away, alarmed by the ruckus and shots. The Kid caught the beast's reins, tossed them to the Mexican.

Their foes were coming at them, shooting and howling like mad wolves. A hundred or more gunmen, brought out by Pecos Durham and Bull McGlone, were massing to the attack.

Bullets cut, blind for the most part, after

them. They heard shrieking lead in the air about them as they rode hell-for-leather south. Slugs plugged dully into the prairie dirt, but within a short time they were zigzagging out of range. Confused yells, the heavy growl of shotguns, more snapping pistols, came from Nauchville, buzzing like a disturbed beehive. Hurriedly gunnies were mounting, to pursue the two who had been spying.

"Head south till we cross the river, then we'll make it back to town," Pryor called, as the jolting of the dun punctuated his speech. Saber was picking up more and more speed. The Kid had to hold him in so that Mireles' animal could stay up.

"Give him the needle, Saber, he's tryin' to cut up," ordered Pryor, as Mireles' beast, caught by a couple of buckshot, began fighting the bit, dancing sideways.

The dun's mirled eye rolled white in his head. As the dark-hided, hammer-headed mustang Mireles forked came abreast, Saber slowing at the Kid's behest, the dun turned his head and bit a chunk of furry hide from the bronc's flank. It straightened the mustang out, and the beast streaked in a bullet line now, mortal fright of the vicious dun making his hoofs fly. Another nip and nothing could have stopped the bullet-headed creature.

They hit the low bank of the Smoky Hill, and splashed through the shallows. Water rose up, whooshing into their faces as the horses crossed. Behind them, a few hundred yards, rode a closely packed gang of pursuers, gunmen eager for their blood.

Back in the Blue Buffalo a man cursed, cursed with the venom of a rattlesnake at Bull McGlone.

"You fool!" he said, voice low. "You missed him! How much and what did he hear? He was up there in the loft — how long? Suppose I hadn't seen him leave Ellsworth, hadn't run on his pet horse here? I was coming to give you orders tonight, you knew that. Where were your guards?"

"Aw, I had a man out back and more in front," Bull McGlone replied defensively. "The boys'll git him. Don't worry."

"I hope so. In any case, someone's got to put him out of the way, and fast. I won't wait any longer."

"Okay, okay, Chief. Tallifero's got it all worked out."

"Pecos Durham's men are in. We'll take control."

"Tonight?"

"We'll start tonight."

The Chief threw himself down in a

wooden chair, reached for the whiskey bottle. His lips writhed over his teeth, in anticipation, as he poured himself a drinking glass full of the belly-burning liquor, downed it without taking the glass from his lips.

He drank another and a third. Bull Mc-Glone watched him in fascination. "I kin drink with the best, Chief," the giant remarked, "but I'd be under the table if I done it like that!"

"Shut up."

Rage burned red from the furious eyes, as the whiskey took effect. But there was no lessening of his faculties. Rather, the rotgut stuff seemed to be his inspiration. He sat bolt upright, glaring straight ahead, hands gripping the edge of the table.

Horsemen were coming back, those whose steeds could not carry them at the breakneck pace set by the fleeing dun.

"What's up, boys?" McGlone asked from the door. "Any luck?"

"Naw," a gunny replied in disgust. "Say, that feller kin fly. He laid out five men at the hosses and they've crossed the river and are headed back. They'll be in town 'fore yuh kin say shucks."

McGlone slammed the door with a curse.

"That Rio Kid's the luckiest devil I ever

111

bucked," he exclaimed.

"His luck's up tonight," the Chief said venomously. "Call Tallifero. The Rio Kid must be buzzard bait 'fore dawn."

McGlone pulled up a chair, sat down and poured a drink.

"We'll buck the town tonight, then," he promised. "Let's have yore ideas, Chief."

The Rio Kid splashed fast across the Smoky Hill River, and headed for the bright lights of Main Street and the plaza. Ellsworth was still wide awake, howling in the night. Foam flecked the powerful, bony dun as Pryor guided Saber up Douglas.

Mireles, a few yards ahead, turned in his saddle.

"You weesh me to stay weeth you, General?"

Slowing the dun, who had certainly done his share of the fighting that night, Pryor replied: "Better go git some shut-eye, Celestino. I'll take up patrol where I left off."

Mireles nodded, raised a brown hand in farewell, cut up a side alley.

The Rio Kid shook blood off his arm, wiped dust and sweat from his hot face. He watered Saber at one of the numerous horse troughs set along the road, then quickly washed himself up, the cool water staunching the bleeding.

He left the dun in front of Jake New's and stalked up on the porch, shoved through the batwing doors. The place was jammed full of rolicking cowboys, hunters and citizens of various ilk. Music was going, drinks passed thick and fast, gamblers at work.

Pryor called for a drink, downed it, rolled himself a brown-paper cigarette. Happy Jack Morco slid up to him.

"Town's mighty quiet, Kid. Don't like it. Usually means hell to pay."

The Rio Kid was thinking things over, what he had overheard of Bull McGlone's and the Syndicate's plans.

"Reckon I better warn Phil Moore," he mused. "They'll be after him tomorrer night if they carry that out."

Drink finished, cigarette curling smoke around his handsome, devil-may-care face, the Rio Kid strolled from New's Saloon out and under the awnings. Cattle cars lined the sidings; the bellowings of the animals were always an undertone to life in Ellsworth.

An Indian, with a full headdress of eagle's feathers, a gay blanket draped on his wide shoulders, came stalking along Main. He was having his first look at a town, and he could hardly believe his black, opaque eyes. A man was quirting a horse in drunken frenzy, and the Kid stepped out, ducking under the hitch-rack to stop the brutality.

"Mind yore bus'ness," snarled the drunk. He raised his quirt, and struck out at the Kid. The marshal's heavy pistol emerged, the barrel cracked on the hombre's skull. He folded up at the Rio Kid's feet, and the Kid dragged the buffaloed one into the shade of a porch and left him there. He had other things to do.

First he went to the home of Mayor Fred Grey. Vern Burnett came sliding from the shadows, buffalo gun in his big hands, as the Rio Kid stepped up on the porch. Grey, following the Kid's advice, had men watching his place day and night.

"That you, Pryor?" demanded Burnett, who could see in the dark.

"Yeah — tell Grey that an attack's goin' to be made on Phil Moore. It's set for to-morrer, but it might be done earlier — now."

"Okay. I'll tell him," promised Burnett.

The Kid nodded, strolled toward Moore's. Phil Moore had a large yard piled high with buffalo hides.

As he approached Moore's, Bat Masterson came along the street.

"Town's mighty tame, Kid," remarked Bat, his frosty, blue eyes disappointed. "Why, it's a lot more excitin' at the 'Dobe Walls. Chief Quanah Parker don't love white men much, 'specially buffalo hunters. He figgers if we keep it up a few years, there'll be no more bison roamin' his plains. Custer put him down last year, but he's risen front the dead. If yuh want some sport, come on down to the Panhandle with us."

"Reckon Ellsworth'll pick up pronto," drawled the Rio Kid.

"S'pose we go buck the Thompsons' game at the Bull's Head," suggested Bat. "Billy's drunk, that allus means excitement."

"I don't need to hunt trouble," laughed the Rio Kid. "Now look, Bat, will yuh b'lieve what I say?"

"Shore," Bat replied quickly, his young brow wrinkling as he tried to figure what was coming.

"Gospel truth?"

"Gospel."

"Then here yuh are: see these nicks I got? Picked 'em up in Nauchville. I wouldn't mention such trivial matters, Bat, but I overheard Bull McGlone's plans as to you buffalo hunters. They're lyin' to yuh, cold and hard. They mean to wipe out ev'ry independent dealer in Kansas. Then they'll pay yuh what they want — a dollar — fifty cents — a hide. Yuh'll take it or not. If yuh don't yore hides rot. As for One-Shot Harry Crane, he's to sign up hunters to work for the Syndicate on salary. What salary will also be up to the Syndicate. In short, if McGlone ain't stopped pronto, he'll own the hide market. He'll buy cheap, and sell dear. Yuh know the hull country's usin' buffalo robes, the beef's sellin' well, and they're makin' the bones into fertilizer."

"Huh," Bat Masterson growled. "I got to tell Hanrahan this."

"Do yuh think he'll take your word for it?"

"Yeah, I think so. But there's thousands of buffalo hunters loose on the plains, Kid."

"That's true. But Hanrahan and yore bunch got a lot of influence. Vern Burnett's with Grey and the independents; if yuh spread word of just what this Syndicate's up to, it'll spoil their game."

"I'll do it. Jim's over in the Grand Central, buckin' the tiger. I'll go find him."

Bat Masterson hustled up the sidewalk. The Rio Kid strolled on till he came to the crude sign marking Moore's Buffalo Mart, fenced high. The board shack at the side, opening on the side alley, was dark, but when the Kid banged on the door with the butt of his gun, he heard someone stirring inside. He also caught the cluck-cluck of a Sharps being cooked and sang out quickly:

"It's Marshal Pryor, Moore. I come to warn yuh."

"What's up?" demanded Phil Moore through the panel.

"I heard McGlone say they're comin' to take yuh over, tomorrer prob'ly, mebbe before. I've told Grey. So watch yoreself."

"Thanks, Kid. What's the matter with coming in and having a drink."

The Rio Kid might have accepted the invitation had he not heard the sudden banging of six-guns in the direction of Jake New's saloon corner.

He ran swiftly from Moore's out into the middle of the wide street. He could look down and see a milling mass of horsemen. Yowls of fury, gunshots split the night air of Ellsworth. Men on the sidewalk were shooting, and the Rio Kid, as town marshal, realized he had a job on his hands.

He jumped inside a saloon, seized a double-barreled shotgun from behind the bar, one he had cached for the purpose, and ran along, starting for the fray.

The Rio Kid, close as had been his shaves with death, had never been so near to the end before, as he charged full-tilt at the melee.

He was almost upon the spot before he suddenly remembered that empty store next to New's Saloon, and the plot of Pete Tallifero.

Chapter XI
The Fight in the Plaza

Quickly the Rio Kid sized up the situation.

What shook him to sudden realization of the game was the angle at which the hombres on the walk and in the road were firing their guns. In such a hot street brawl, men full of red liquor would not be so careful to aim at the sky. His quick eyes, trained to size up fighting groups, took in the angled flashes of the six-guns from the walk. The horsemen, too, though jerking their mustangs around, and yowling, were also deliberately firing high.

The Rio Kid stopped, heels digging into the dust. He whirled, turning away from the fighting mob. The empty store next to Jake New's lowered at him and he saw the raised sash of a black window. As he turned, a Sharps buffalo gun, sending a slug of lead that weighed eight to the pound, with a charge of powder behind it powerful enough to stop a charging fifteen-hundred-pound bull dead in his tracks, whooshed its horrible, deep roar of death.

That bullet, half an inch in diameter, two inches long, would tear the soul out of a man. The wind of its passing was almost stunning. He saw the great flash of exploding powder. Pete Tallifero had made his play. Only the Kid's sudden pause and changing direction had kept the great slug from finishing his career.

"The great blessin' of a Sharps, when it's against yuh," thought the Kid, "is that it's a single shot!"

Hardly had the huge gun roared at him, than the Rio Kid's shotgun snapped answer. The buckshot was half scattered as it struck the window. Tallifero, sighting along the Sharps, evidently took some of them in the face, for he let out a scream of anguish and the rifle, released from his hands, rattled on the window sill, no longer supported.

Shouts of fury came from the throats of the supposed fighters. Horsemen whirled their mounts, the broncs fighting the bits, rearing, as their riders spurred them toward the Kid, their six-shooters talking.

But the lithe Pryor no longer stood in the road. He ran to the door of the empty store, banged it in with his shoulder, jumping into the dark interior. He heard Pete Tallifero cursing a blue streak to his left. There was an open doorway into a large room, and the Kid was inside, leaning his shotgun against the wall.

"Tallifero!" snarled the Rio Kid.

Pete Tallifero heard him, knew who it was.

"Damn yuh, yuh near put out my eye —" he howled.

The snaky devil fell suddenly to his knee, and the Rio Kid, in the blackness of the interior, heard the whip that a gun makes when it leaves leather. He stepped aside, his own Colt flashing out into his expert hand. Tallifero's first one from his revolver bit at the Kid's cheek, burrowed into the wooden partition behind him. An instant-fraction later and the Kid pinned the blue-yellow gun flare dead center, aiming as a man points his forefinger.

He shot a second time, on the breath of the first, just to make sure — Tallifero was already sinking.

Swiftly the Rio Kid glided to the corpse, gun up in case Tallifero were shamming. But the snaky breed had taken both bullets in the breast; he was dead before he stopped rolling. The Rio Kid struck a match, cupped it in his left hand to make certain.

Blood seeped from the bullet holes in Tallifero's shirt and vest. A howl of fury came from outside, and someone shot through the window glass, sending more of it tinkling to the floor; the Kid's buckshot had smashed and cracked it before. They aimed at his match, and the slug burnt his leg as he hastily dropped the burning stick and jumped away, seizing his shotgun.

He heard Pecos Durham bawling: "Hey, Pete, hold him — hold him, Pete, we're comin'."

"Damn right yuh're comin'," snarled the Kid, "comin' right after Tallifero!"

Fighting blood high, he sent his second load from the shotgun into the bunched killers, Pecos Durham's gang. Yelps of pain, the cursing of them as they fell back, rang in the empty building. The Kid ducked for the back way, found it, ran out into Tin Can Alley, and hotfooted it for New's rear door. He had another shotgun waiting, and exchanged it for the empty one.

So terrific was the roar of the conflict that it began to draw more than local interest. All of Ellsworth dropped what it was doing. The timid and those who had no desire to take part in such affairs, ducked or hid; the more curious peeped from windows or from behind water barrels and posts.

The Rio Kid, darting on through Jake New's, picked up Happy Jack Morco, who was hustling out, a double-barreled shotgun in one hand.

"What's up, is Clay Allison in town with his pards?"

'Nope — Pecos Durham, and some friends of McGlone's — tried to take me. I just downed Pete Tallifero next door."

Most of Pecos Durham's gunnies had rushed for the vacant store in which Tallifero's bullet-riddled corpse lay in a pool of blood. Some of them were firing at shadows inside the building. Others were riding up and down, cursing and shooting off their pistols to cow any organization of resistance.

From up Main, where stood Phil Moore's big hide yard, more guns began to pop. The Rio Kid, sliding out of the saloon with Happy Jack at his heels, caught the flare of those guns. He also noted that heavy resistance burst from the fence and shack, knew that Fred Grey must have come up to assist Moore.

Having executed his swift doubling movement, the Rio Kid threw up his shotgun, covering the bunched hombres of Pecos Durham. He noted the big, rawboned leader, Durham himself, a man with a florid complexion, a face so freckled that not even a hide bug could have found a spot to stand on without having at least one foot on a blotch, and evil, red-sparkling eyes under the black Stetson. Durham, husky and broad, was bellowing commands in a buffalo bull's voice.

"I'll get that red-headed shark from the Pecos," the Rio Kid told Happy Jack.

Many things began to happen. As the Kid maneuvered along the walk for a fair shot at Pecos Durham, Bat Masterson, six-guns visible, came rocketing out of the Grand Central and galloped across the plaza. Vern Burnett's tall figure, a Sharps buffalo gun in his big paws, was running toward the Rio Kid. Marshal Ed Hogue, up at the other end of town, was also on his way to the heart of the trouble.

"Durham!" roared the Rio Kid, voice cracking with military sharpness over the intermittent banging of guns.

Pecos Durham heard him, and turned in his leather, Colt rising.

"There he is — git him," he bellowed, and pointed with his pistol muzzle at the marshal. Aiming a Frontier Model Colt was the same as pointing a forefinger.

The redhead's hogleg flared, but the bullet dug into the sidewalk two yards in front of the Rio Kid. The shotgun in his steady

123

hands roared, and the spreading charge caught Pecos Durham in the head. Blood spurted from a dozen tearing wounds. Durham's face was a horrible mask as he let go of his weapons and clawed at his blinded eyes.

The wolfish desperadoes who had given allegiance to the man from the Pecos swung their guns on the Rio Kid. Pecos Durham was dying, he fell off his horse, but one foot stayed in the stirrup and the wild black mustang, which had taken several of the scattering pellets, rushed pell-mell across the railroad tracks, dragging what was left of the outlaw after him.

The Rio Kid jumped for the water barrel set between New's and the vacant store in which he had finished Tallifero. He shoved a spectator back out of his way, and opened up with the second barrel of his shotgun, buckshot peppering the gunnies massing toward him.

Bat Masterson, who had seen the Kid in action, crouched at the side of a freight car, and began shooting into the gunmen horde. Vern Burnett's buffalo gun roared death as the tall, somber-eyed hunter picked out the enemy. Marshal Happy Jack Morco and Marshal Ed Hogue were diving into the action, shotguns roaring.

The gunnies who had been hunting the vacant store for the Rio Kid came charging out, leaped on their horses, held ready by their mates, and the whole gang, shooting six-guns back, rode hell-for-leather west in the middle of the wide street. The Rio Kid, dropping his shotgun, drew two six-shooters, and, one in each hand, jumped out into the gutter and followed them with his lead.

The ruckus had stopped at Moore's. Vague, dark figures were hastily retreating eastward along Tin Can Alley, headed for Nauchville.

But Pecos Durham's killers, wheeling at the end of the building lines, came whooping and shooting back up Main Street. The Rio Kid, spine to the line of buildings, worked his six-guns with the speed of light. Forty-five slugs blasted the gunny lines, two flew from their galloping mustangs, others turned and left the bunch. Morco, Hogue, and others were assisting. The Kid, from the corner of his eye, saw the slender figure of Celestino Mireles as the Mexican lad charged up, firing a Winchester rifle.

The instants were ticking off. The Rio Kid would not give ground. Bullets were zipping past him, smashing windows, tearing great splinters from the sidewalk and porches. He

felt the clutching death as it ventilated his
Stetson and ripped holes in his clothes.

He was hit, not once but several times,
stinging paths left by the bullets bloody
wakes. A slug tore off one of his high-boot
heels. The whole howling mob of murderous gunmen swerved in at the marshal.

Then a dozen hombres came running up
Main Street. They were Fred Grey's hide
dealers, who had just driven off Bull Mc-
Glone's drygulchers at Moore's yard. They
had rifles and they jumped instantly into
the fray. A fusillade cut the flank of the
charging gunnies, and half a dozen died. So
terrific was the onslaught, fronted by the
guns of the Rio Kid, that the killers quailed.
No man in the hard-riding gang wanted to
be in front, where one after another was
shot from the back of his mustang. They
veered away, and in a few seconds went on
past, riding full-tilt for Nauchville.

The Rio Kid limped out into the middle
of Ellsworth plaza, both hot guns smoking
in his bronzed hands. Blood trickled from a
scalp crease and from a jagged gash in his
cheek where a bullet had furrowed. There
was a hole in the flesh of his calf, laming
him. His clothes were shot to ribbons.

Bloody but with guns up and victory in
his glinting, devil-may-care blue eyes, the

Rio Kid, marshal of Ellsworth, shouted his warcry as the gunnies of the deceased Pecos Durham rode off in ignominious defeat.

Chapter XII
"All Is Quiet in Ellsworth"

Ellsworth now seemed at peace. The sun of a new day shone benignly down on the plaza, on the very wide Main Street. On the K.P. tracks a freight train of sixty cattle cars was being shunted to the loading position by a noisy but businesslike steam engine. Steers bellowed plaintively. Cattlemen, sobered up from the night before, were prodding their charges, with curses of relief after months of coddling on the Texas Trail, into the chutes.

Trade went on. Women in sun bonnets and bright gingham dresses were at the various marts, children clinging to their bustles, market baskets filling.

The bodies from the terrible gunfight of the night before had been picked up in a wagon and dumped into a grave dug at Boot Hill.

In the dirt where men had lost their lives,

the stains were already being covered by fresh-risen dust of horses and wagons, of beating hoofs and feet.

ALL IS QUIET IN ELLSWORTH!

read the headline in the Ellsworth *Reporter.* Under this, the *Reporter,* to whom death was a commonplace, had several snappy items. One was headed:

ELLSWORTH'S NEW MARSHAL CHRISTENS MAIN STREET!

Then, in smaller type:

Marshal Bob Pryor, known to his pards as "The Rio Kid," had a slight argument with about a hundred gunmen under the leadership of one Pecos Durham, supposed badman from Texas way — H'yah, Texas, welcome to our city! Don't forget Jake New sells the biggest glass of whiskey in town, or so he paid us to say here.

Marshal Pryor, who was taking a quiet stroll along the main thoroughfare of our glorious Buffalo and Steer Metropolis, chanced to observe the rudeness of Mr. Durham's celebrations. As the Marshal sorrowfully chided Mr. Durham, a few hundred bullets strayed his way. After he had dodged a bellyful, Marshal Pryor began shooting. Ably assisted by his side men, Marshals Morco and Hogue and by the artistic six-shooter manipulations of Mr. Bat Masterson, at the moment in our midst, Marshal Pryor chased the funsters out of town.

P.S. Eight dead and about seventeen wounded, far as we can guess!

Another item, right under the big black letters that spelled

QUIET

Pete Tallifero, better known as Pete the Feet, was found shot dead in Fanner's vacant store (For rent, 10 pilasters per month) last night. It seems Mr. Tallifero's finger slipped and Marshal Pryor, thinking Mr. Tallifero was trying to blow his spine through his lungs, was justly indignant, more so at Mr. Tallifero's *faux-pas* (that's Latin for missing) in aiming so poorly than at the implied expression of dislike, shot him first with about thirty (30) buckshot and next with his Colt's .45. (Ammunition by Keeler's Hardware Store. Best in Kansas.) This morning Marshal Pryor is mourning the waste of good .45 shells because the buckshot would have done amply. Those wishing to see the remains of Mr. Tallifero, apply Boot Hill, Ellsworth, Kansas.

On a cot, upstairs in the back of the Grand Central, lay the Rio Kid. Celestino Mireles, tender as a woman, sat close at hand. He had helped bind up the Kid's injuries, watched over him as he slept. Waking to the fresh sunlight, the Kid was stiff, wounds aching. He grunted, reached for the "makin's" to fix himself a smoke, but Mireles beat him to it, rolled him a brown-paper cylinder which the Kid smoked with deep relish.

"General," Celestino said, dark eyes worried, "you hav' narrow es-cape! You should nevaire hav' stood in ze street so."

The Rio Kid grinned, shrugged, then grimaced with the pain of the movement.

"Huh. Don't reckon they'll try to hurrah the town thataway again, Celestino. Say, I'm hungry. Anything to eat in this burg?"

The lean Mexican lad hustled from the room. Resting his wounds, the Kid waited. He ate the hearty breakfast Celestino fetched from the restaurant downstairs.

"General," Mireles said, when he had finished, "ze may-or weeshes to spik weeth

130

you. Also Senor Weelkins. Zey wait below."

"Well, tell 'em to come up," the Rio Kid ordered.

Propped up, the Kid grinned at Frey Grey and florid Sam Wilkins, leaders of the Independent Dealers.

"How are you, Pryor?" Wilkins asked.

"Oh, feelin' okay," drawled the Kid. "Did yuh stop that attack on Phil Moore all right last night?"

"Sure, sure," Grey replied with a satisfied air. "I figger we've busted that Syndicate's back, Pryor, thanks to yuh. McGlone's gone, and so're Pecos Durham's riders. Can't find hide nor hair of 'em in Nauchville or here. They say they rode toward Dodge City, left word they're through here. And this mornin' Jim Hanrahan told Harry Crane, the Syndicate's chief of hunters, to go to hell. Hanrahan says his friends mean to sell to us, no matter what price the Syndicate claims to offer."

Good, the Rio Kid thought. His play had worked. Bat Masterson had convinced the slow-spoken, influential Hanrahan of the Syndicate's perfidy.

"That's fine," the Kid said. "Others will foller their lead. I reckon the Syndicate won't take as many hides as they expected."

"You're right," Sam Wilkins agreed.

131

"You've sure worked miracles, Pryor. Mc-Glone's gone, maybe for good. Ellsworth looks a lot safer than it did this time yesterday."

"Hanrahan's party is pullin' out at dawn tomorrer mornin'," explained Grey.

"How's the new marshal this mornin'." The slow-spoken, ironical voice came from the door.

Bob Pryor turned his eyes that way, saw the handsome Bat Masterson laughing in at him.

"C'mon in, Bat."

"Hanrahan's through with the Syndicate. Bob," Masterson said. "I convinced him yuh're right. We're sellin' to Grey and his friends. Now look. Yuh've cleaned up Ellsworth, McGlone's gone and his gunnies with him. Why not throw in with us and come buffalo huntin' to the Panhandle? We got our wagonloads of supplies headin' for the 'Dobe Walls. This'll be the biggest hunt yet."

The Rio Kid laughed, shook his head.

"I reckon I'll stick around town a while longer, Bat. But thanks just the same."

The Rio Kid was not yet satisfied with the way things had gone. Behind Bull McGlone was someone, the "Chief," whom he had not yet identified. That had to be done

132

before there could be any permanent peace. Besides, he was tired from the terrific battles of the past days. He wanted to rest up, get his breath.

There was still another reason. Down the street lived Miss Ruth Grey. The Kid was more interested in her than he would admit.

"Ruth's worried 'bout yuh," said Grey. "She gave me quite a talkin' to for not makin' yuh come over to the house after yuh was wounded. S'posin' we git a stretcher and fetch yuh there now?"

The Kid grinned, sat up, and stood on his two pins. He teetered a bit but drew himself erect.

"I guess I kin still use my feet," he drawled, "when I git a new boot heel."

"Then come on over and have a drink," Grey said.

Celestino hovered near his pard, afraid the Kid might fall. But Pryor, the power of youth overcoming his injuries, was already on the mend.

Ruth was in the front door of the Grey home, Vern Burnett behind her. She greeted the Kid with a cry of joy, touched his hand.

"I'm so grateful," she whispered. "You did it, alone, Bob. You cleaned them out of town."

The Rio Kid was deeply affected by the

soft touch of the young woman. Her forth-
right eyes sought his, and for a moment they
looked at one another. Then she dropped
her gaze, flushing a little. Vern Burnett,
somber eyes veiled, swung on his heels,
walked out the back way.

The Kid took an armchair.

"I dunno how safe yuh are as yet, Grey,"
he drawled. "It's a little early, seems to me,
to burn up our guns. McGlone's still kickin'
and so are a bunch of other sidewinders."

"They won't come back," Wilkins said
confidently.

Ellsworth was really quiet that day. There
was no shooting in the town that night.
Decorum and good manners seemed to
prevail. The Rio Kid, sitting in Jake New's
saloon, had no cause to sally forth. Happy
Jack Morco and Ed Hogue easily handled
the town.

Mireles had disappeared again, on one of
his periodical forays. The Kid figured the
Mexican lad had gone to Nauchville, there
to sound out his acquaintances for news of
Bull McGlone.

Another night's sleep, and the Kid felt like
a new man. He was still limping a bit, but
his wounds were healing rapidly. In the red
of the dawn, the sun a huge ruby ball seem-
ing to touch the eastern prairie, Bob Pryor

said good-by to Bat Masterson and Jim Hanrahan, the buffalo hunters. A long train of wagons, driven by skinners for the hunters, most of them Mexicans, and accompanied by hard-eyed, grim-faced frontiersmen mounted on their mustangs, started south out of Ellsworth.

The Rio Kid walked along beside Masterson's stirrup. As they came abreast of Fred Grey's, Ruth called to them from the porch.

"Oh, Mr. Masterson — have you seen Vern Burnett this morning?"

Mr. Masterson swept off the gray sombrero, on which the gold-and-silver rattlesnake band gleamed in the morning sunlight.

"No, Ma'am," he replied gallantly, and his horse, Houston, danced a bow before the pretty girl. "But I'll tell him yuh was askin' after him next I see him. *Adios,* Ma'am."

Bat Masterson took his leave of Miss Grey, backing Houston away and falling into line after the flat wagons of his pals.

The Kid stepped up on the porch.

"Yuh don't know where Vern is?" he inquired.

"No." She shook her trim head, eyes filled with worry. "In fact, I didn't see him at all yesterday, Bob. His horse is gone and so is he. I can't understand it."

The Rio Kid stared at her. He knew of Burnett's jealousy of himself. He guessed that the young fellow, unable to stand the pain of it longer, had saddled his horse and ridden into the wilderness. Vern Burnett was that kind of a man. He would not have left while there seemed to be need of him.

"He shore must love her," he mused. Looking at Ruth, he couldn't blame Burnett.

He felt that way himself.

But Bob Pryor, formerly a dashing cavalry captain in the Grand Army of the Republic, was more worldly-wise than young Burnett, whose experience had been solely that of the frontier. The Kid knew women. He had, in fact, been in love before or had believed himself to be. Ruth Grey attracted him strongly. She was beautiful, she was clever, and a wonderful girl.

But on the other hand there were various other interests affecting the Rio Kid.

Footloose and fancy free as he had been, driven to his wanderings by the devastation and chaos of the great Civil War, he did not feel capable of settling down to the tameness of home and fireside.

And as he watched the girl's puzzled eyes, the way she kept turning from him to look down or up the wide street of Ellsworth for

some sign of Vern Burnett, the Rio Kid
steeled himself.

"He'll be back, Ma'am," he said. "No
doubt he's rode on to 'Dobe Walls." Turning, he swung away, back to the Grand
Central, where his quarters were.

Chapter XIII
Flight

The day passed quietly. Dark came, and
with it Celestino Mireles, riding in, silently,
stealthily. The slim Mexican slid up to Pryor
outside the saloon.

"General," he said, "McGlone ees back."

"Huh! Yuh see him?"

"*Si*. Crane ees not weeth him. Zey plan
somezing, General. I mus' stay in Nauchville. I am hide zere."

"Okay. But be careful," warned the Kid.
"Is McGlone at the Blue Buffalo?"

"No, he hide somewhere else. He ees in
touch weeth his gunmen, I know zat."

Warned by the Mexican, the Rio Kid kept
a sharp eye peeled for McGlone. But there
was no trouble that night. He watched a big
cowman from Texas celebrating the sale of
a herd of five thousand beeves.

The rancher was prodigal with his roll,

big enough to choke a steer. Drinks were on Big Joe Pembroke.

The Kid accepted a couple of free drinks, and talked briefly with the big, bluff Texan. He had heard of Pembroke on the Border.

Everybody saw the thousands of dollars carried by Pembroke in his roll. It was freely exhibited and eyes gleamed with cupidity, with envy.

The Kid went on, patroling the town for signs of trouble. He stopped a drunken fight, took away a laughing madman's pistols as the rollicking son of Texas sought to hurrah the settlement, locking the waddy up until he should be sober.

It was not long until Big Jim Pembroke sought him out, the rancher trailed by a dozen of his cowboys.

"Looka here, Marshal," growled Pembroke. "Yuh got one of my boys in yore calaboose. Leave him go, savvy?"

"No hard feelin's, Pembroke," drawled the Rio Kid pacifically. "Yore man was endangerin' folks' lives. He was too drunk for his own good. I'll let him loose in the mornin' and he kin ride back to yore camp."

Pembroke scowled. "Now looka. Tonight's a big night, Marshal. Yuh nawthern peace officers pick on us cowmen too damn often.

I'll take my bus'ness to Dodge City after this."

The Kid shrugged. "Yuh're wrong, Pembroke. I come from the Rio Grande country myself. I saved yore man from gittin' plugged."

Drunk as he was, Big Jim Pembroke was a fair and square fellow. He scowled at the Rio Kid, but then he shrugged.

"Okay, but yuh let him ride back to camp in the mornin' or I'll come in and git him."

The Kid finished his night's work as dawn touched the eastern sky. He retired to the Grand Central and turned in.

In the afternoon he went out, rode Saber for several miles to exercise the dun. It was dark again when they returned to Ellsworth. He left the dun saddled, thinking he might ride later on, if all was quiet.

He ate supper in the restaurant next to the courthouse, then strolled back along the crowded street.

When he came to the Grand Central, he went upstairs to his room to get some shells for his shotguns. He washed up, changed his shirt, whistling to himself.

Celestino Mireles appeared in the door.

"General," Mireles cried, "queeck, no time to lose! You mus' leav' town."

"What's up?" demanded the Kid.

139

"McGlone — he plan somezing agains' you, but I can't say what. A man was keel las' night, a beeg ranchero — Pembroke —"

"What's that got to do with me?"

Heavy steps sounded on the wooden stairs leading to the second story, where the Kid's room was located.

"C'mon — c'mon, General," whispered Mireles despairingly. "Please — come weeth me —"

Men were crowding in the hallway, but they had not yet appeared in the door. They stopped before they showed, and a gruff voice sang out:

"Pryor! I wanta talk to yuh."

"Who's that?" answered the Kid. His guns, taken off as he changed his shirt and washed up, lay in their belt on the cot. He sidled over so he could reach them.

"It's Tazewell. Ben Tazewell, sheriff of Ellsworth County, Pryor. I got my posse with me. Throw out yore guns, and be keer-ful how yuh move. I'm a-comin' in!"

"Come ahead," the Kid told him. "Nothin' to be afeared of, Tazewell." He had heard of the county official. Tazewell was said to be a good man and a quick one with a gun.

A grizzled hombre in a sweated brown Stetson, a sheriff's star pinned to his vest, stuck his head around the doorway. He had a six-shooter in his hand. Celestino Mireles stood silently behind the door.

There were many men behind Tazewell, not from Ellsworth but from surrounding parts. Some were cowmen, others citizens of smaller camps. The sheriff had brought them along. Also, the Rio Kid recognized a couple of Big Jim Pembroke's cowboys.

One of the latter pointed at the Kid.

"That's the man, Sheriff! He shot Pembroke, took his roll, and gunned us. I got a bullet through the arm. He had some pals with him."

Angrily he held up his bandaged wrist.

"Yuh're lyin', cowboy," drawled the Kid.

Tazewell scowled. He had a stern, heavily lined face, brown goatee and long mustache touched with gray hairs.

"No use tryin' to buffalo us, Pryor. I got a warrant for yore arrest, signed by Jedge Newbold Lask. Two witnesses saw yuh down Pembroke last night, just outside of town as he was on his way back to his camp."

"McGlone's behind this, I reckon," the Rio Kid said. "Yuh're makin' a big mistake, Sheriff —" He shifted, not with hostile intention, but so he could take in the pressing crowd behind the officer.

However, the slight movement he made

alarmed Tazewell. The sheriff thought he was going for his guns. With lightning rapidity, and skillful, expert motion, Tazewell's Frontier Model Colt covered the Rio Kid.

The sheriff kept his eyes on the Kid, but he called back over his shoulder, "Step inside, Brownie, and search him."

A squat deputy with a face brown as a baked cake shoved in, and quickly frisked the Rio Kid, who stood, still unable to figure out exactly what was occuring.

"Nuthin' much on him, Sheriff."

"Well, keep lookin', keep lookin'," Ben Tazewell ordered impatiently. "A man don't allus carry a roll on his hide."

Brownie searched. He pulled back the straw mattress of the Rio Kid's cot.

"Huh," he cried. "here 'tis, Sheriff. Looks like he hid it in a hurry."

He raised on high a roll of bills and a black leather wallet.

"That's Pembroke's," exclaimed the cowboy. "And some of his money's there. I told yuh, Sheriff, we both heard Pryor's pards call him by name durin' the holdup."

Too late, the Rio Kid savvied the game. Tazewell might be honest, might simply be an innocent tool of the Syndicate, which had arranged this frame-up. It was a neat one. The Kid had even had a little tiff with the rancher the night before. He decided that McGlone must have fixed up one of his men to look enough like the Kid to fool the cowboys with Pembroke in the darkness. A hint or two would cinch it in their minds.

Now the gun was on him. He could not fight without injuring the posse-men and the sheriff, whom he believed honest.

He also knew that once disarmed and helpless in the town lock-up, he would be as good as dead. Even if Bull McGlone didn't bring a lynch mob, he would be hung for the carefully planted crime. Judge Lask would help — McGlone and his men, lying witnesses, the Pembroke cowboys.

The posse in the hall surged forward. At that instant a cool, level voice spoke from behind the door, which was pushed nearly against the wall.

"Drop ze gun, Shereef, and reach!"

Celestino Mireles had Ben Tazewell covered from the flank.

The shock of it, for he had not before seen the Mexican lad, made Tazewell gasp a curse, but he let his pistol drop, metallic thud on the floor. Mireles had him pinned. The sheriff could not shoot without turning. The fierce black eyes, the hawklike nose, the curved lips of the Mexican were witness to his determination.

"Yuh better put down that gun, boy," blustered Tazewell.

The Rio Kid, the instant the sheriff's gun was off him, snatched up his own weapons, buckled on his belt. Tazewell and the wounded cowboy stood between Pryor and the posse outside. They dared not start shooting without orders from the sheriff, and Tazewell figured he would be first to die.

Pryor slipped aside, taking his stand by Mireles, gun up.

"Back out into the hall, Sheriff," he drawled. "Don't want to hurt yuh."

Tazewell was glad to obey; he backed outside. The Kid slammed the door. He and Celestino exited through the window.

They dodged through Tin Can Alley, where the Mexican youth seized his mustang's dropped reins.

"Tak' my horse, es-cape, General," he cried.

But the Rio Kid whistled piercingly.

In answer, Saber, eyes rolling, galloped up. The Kid hit leather in a bound and, stretched low along the dun, beat it on south. Bullets and horsemen streamed after him out of Ellsworth. Hell-for-leather the two rode, the dun's flying hoofs picking up space on the pursuit. The Rio Kid, a short while before the man of the hour, the tin god of Ellsworth, now was a hunted fugitive with a murder cinched on him, a warrant out for his arrest dead or alive, on the dodge. Pryor chuckled at the irony of it.

The Rio Kid looked back over his shoulder at the town. A reckless smile touched his lips; angry as he was inside, danger was tonic to him.

"Look out, General!" screamed Celestino.

A bunch of burly, masked hombres spurted out, half a dozen of them riding across their path. The Mexican's gun blazed into them. One crashed. The Rio Kid's Colts were barking as he swung to face them, gunnies of Bull McGlone. The giant was in the background, crying: "Kill him — shoot him dead —"

Three of Bull McGlone's hombres were down. The rest broke, horses rearing or plunging from the path of the biting, furious dun, the Colts of the Rio Kid.

McGlone was firing a Winchester, its explosions whiplike in sound, as fast as he could pump in bullets. The Rio Kid swung as he passed through the scattered gang, pistol aiming toward the bulk that was McGlone.

At that moment something got him in the

head, stunning, overpowering. He fought against the stupefying blackness that descended, lights flashing across his blinded eyes, ears roaring. He fell forward in his saddle. The iron grip of his legs was still on his leather, by instinct. The dun whirled on, and Mireles kept shooting back at the foe, the senseless Rio Kid on Saber galloping at the Mexican's flank.

Chapter XIV
The Buffalo Hunters

Vern Burnett pushed his big horse out of the thicket of cottonwoods fringing the Canadian River, which flowed eastward through the Texas Panhandle.

That dust in the sky to the north, hanging like a cloud over this vast flat land, had told him a wagon train was coming, and watching for a time, he had recognized his friends, Jim Hanrahan's party of buffalo men.

He had been waiting for them, intending to join the hunt. His heart was aching in his breast, he was in mental pain. He had faced all sorts of danger, privation. Indians, enemies who fired on him, but he did not know how to face what had come upon him since he had met Ruth Grey. He had fallen

146

in love with the level-eyed beauty of Ellsworth. He had hoped, for a time, that he might win her. But the Rio Kid had proved the better man. So Vern Burnett had silently thrown his warbags over his horse and ridden out of Ellsworth.

Camping in the wilderness, on the Great Plains, he had avoided settlements and ranches. His rifle provided him with buffalo meat, with deer, with partridge or other game. He could hit a squirrel in either eye from two hundred yards.

His course was toward the Canadian River.

Adobe Walls, the little outpost where the buffalo hunters might deposit their hides and pick up fresh ammunition and supplies from Jim Hanrahan and Bob Wright, lay on the north bank of the river, fringing the Llano Estacado or Staked Plain. Vern knew the history of the terrible flatlands, dry for mile on mile. Across it had strode the Jesuit fathers, in the centuries before. They had been forced to set up stakes to guide them in that monotonous wilderness. Comanches, Cheyennes, Arapahoes, Kiowas, rode their hairy mustangs bareback on their raids across the Staked Plain. Here they had fought and hunted buffalo for generations, lords of the wilderness until the white man came in.

Vern had not gone up the stream to Adobe Walls, but had camped down river to await the arrival of his friends. He had to be alone for a time, fighting against what had so hurt him.

Burnett let his horse go at its own gait, riding out to meet the oncoming train. Wagons, their axles creaking, drawn by mules and plugs, were strung out for two miles, some that had broken down or bogged in stream fords being a distance behind the rest. Along the line rode the buffalo hunters, Sharps in leather slings, pistols belted and ready. All carried long knives sharp as razors. They wore buckskin as a rule, and they allowed their hair to grow in luxuriant length. The purpose of the latter was not so much the absence of barbers on the range but to keep the good opinion of Indians, who considered a man who trimmed his hair short a cheat. A thick growth of hair meant a man was not afraid to flaunt his scalp and induced highest respect in the redman's heart.

Here came Bat Masterson, mounted on Houston, his pet buckskin, with Marie, the big buffalo gun, lovingly tended. The pantherlike Bat, lithe and with terrific drive, was burned to brown crispness. His cold, light-blue eyes flicked from one side to the other, watching the horizons for signs of marauders.

The hunters presented an aspect of strength that was overpowering. Bronzed and hard of eye, capable to the point of genius with guns, absolutely fearless, the buffalo hunter was one of the toughest men in history.

Jim Hanrahan, the big Irishman who was a leader among these individualists, slouched in his saddle, a leathery cheek bulged by a cud of tobacco. Here rode Billy Dixon, Bermuda Carlisle, Bob Wright, old Man Keeler, Billy Ogg, and a dozen other men famous throughout the West as pioneers, hunters and scouts.

They recognized Burnett from afar. Bat Masterson, who was a special friend of Vern's, both being the same age, spurred Houston out to greet him.

"Why, yuh old tarantula," cried Bat, reaching out from horseback to grasp Burnett's big hand. "Thought yuh'd haided for the Rio Grande or mebbe hell! What the tarnation happened to yuh in Ellsworth? Ev'rybuddy was lookin' for yah, Vern. That little lady —"

Bat broke off, bit his lip, catching the tightening of Burnett's grim face. He shut up on the subject of Ruth Grey.

Riding ahead of the caravan, the two young fellows turned along the Canadian and swung west toward Adobe Walls, where they were to take part in the greatest of Indian fights, although as yet neither had an inkling of what was brewing.

For fifteen hundred miles, from far into Texas up to Canada, and five hundred miles across, the buffalo grass formed a thick, nutritious mat of fodder for the migrating herds. Millions on millions of the shaggy creatures moved southward in regular cycles, following the weather seasons. Each spring as grass grew fresh the buffalo moved north, spending the summer in the Dakotas, Montana and Canada. When cold weather began up north, they swung south to winter in Kansas, The Nations, and Texas. During the southward migration they grew their winter coats and thus were more valuable to the hide hunters from September to March.

Outfitting in the Kansas settlements, great numbers of hunters would intercept the herds in Nebraska and follow them to the Panhandle, killing as they went.

The men in Hanrahan's train were experts. They were out to kill as many animals as possible and get the hides to market for money. The wild ways of early Indian hunters, and the mad riding of the Wild West show-offs, who would gallop a mustang at full speed with the buffalo, shooting them on the hoof, was derided by such professionals. They shot from a stand, hidden behind a sagebrush clump, skillfully dropping first the leaders, and keeping their kill grouped in a small area so their skinners would have an easier time of it and not miss any dead ones as would have been the case had the beasts been scattered over miles of country.

It was late that afternoon when Vern Burnett and Bat Masterson rode up to Adobe Walls, the isolated outpost of the buffalo hunters. Low hills domed the shallow valley in which it stood, three rude structures of adobe bricks feet thick, and loopholed, well back from the Canadian thickets.

The chief of the shacks was Hanrahan's saloon. A man named Kimball ran a rude blacksmith shop which did vital work in shoeing horses against the stony plains. This sort of underfooting had proved disastrous to camels the government had brought from Africa before the war to run mail and army supplies across the American deserts. The camels, used to the soft Sabara sands, could not carry packs here, and had been turned loose. Now and then a hunter, out on the Staked Plain, would sight one of the wild, ungainly beasts.

Bob Wright's store was the third building of Adobe Walls. The store traded with red and white hunters, taking skins for calico, flour, whiskey, guns and bullets, coffee, sugar and gee-gaws. Adobe Walls was a far run from Dodge City, nearest civilization, two hundred miles from nowhere. The hunters did not remain there, but usually there would be ten to twenty around the place during the season.

The air on the high prairies was like wine, bracing, sweet with aromatic scents. The Canadian ran in its tree-fringed cut, soft waters splashing over stony bed. Inside Mr. Hanrahan's saloon a well had been dug, despite the proximity of the river water. Mr. Hanrahan was a man of deep cunning and caution was part of his makeup. People sometimes laughed at the well, but the time might come, Jim Hanrahan would say, when they would laugh on the other side of their mouths.

Three times a day meals were served in Hanrahan's, community affairs where everybody reached for what he desired.

Bat Masterson and Vern Burnett dismounted at the saloon, strolled into the crude, semi-dark structure with quick steps.

"Howdy, gents." The hail came from a big man in buckskin, a pipe clenched between his teeth. There were a dozen more around, silent, heavily armed hombres, apparently occupied with their drinks.

Bat Masterson paused, on the lips of his toes. He was on balance, ready for anything. Vern Burnett leaned his big figure against the door frame; both Bat and Vern had their Sharps rifles in hand, for it was seldom they left their guns behind when outside a settlement.

"Why, good evenin', Harry," drawled Bat.

His icy blue eyes, fixed and steady, were on the hard face of One-Shot Harry Crane. Burnett, too, watched the Hide Syndicate's chief of buffalo hunters from under veiled lashes. From Crane, if there was to be any trouble, would come the signal.

But Crane kept both hands in sight. His buffalo gun leaned against the adobe wall behind him, his pistols were holstered. He smiled in friendly fashion.

"Step up and have a drink, boys. They're on me."

"Didn't reckon yuh'd be down this way," Bat remarked.

Masterson was a friendly soul. Tough as he was, he did not hunt for gun-fights.

Crane, though he had a reputation as a rough customer, was not an outlaw to Kansas. A man's past was his own, it was how he behaved at the moment that counted. The hombres with One-Shot Harry looked like hunters and skinners. Bat knew some of them, casually, having seen them in Dodge and other camps.

"Where yuh keep yore wagons?" asked Burnett suddenly.

"Huh?" Crane said. He glanced into Burnett's eyes for a moment, then smiled again. "Why, Burnett, we figger on huntin' nawthwest of here. Sorta thought we'd try Rabbit Ear. Left our Mexes and wagons twenty mile off, in a hidden draw. But we was short of tobacco and liquor and rode down to pick some up."

"Hanrahan will be in soon," Bat told Crane. "He's got plenty of fresh supplies."

One-Shot Harry Crane said nothing about the break between Hanrahan's party and the Hide Syndicate. Burnett disliked Crane, but kept it to himself. From Fred Grey's story he knew that Crane had been with McGlone when they had tried to kill Ruth's father, and the Rio Kid had come between them and their prey. He contemplated picking a fight with Crane, but the latter gave him no opportunity. He was smooth and

154

good-humored, offering to buy drinks.

The rest of the hunters straggled up, pulling their wagons into a circle around the tiny camp. Hanrahan, cud bulging his cheek, spat as he came in the door, and nodded to Crane and the others.

Vern went over and sat down by himself. Bat Masterson was occupied in checking over some ammunition he had brought out from Kansas.

None of the hunters felt the slightest quiver of worry over the presence of Crane and his silent crew. They could take care of themselves. One-Shot Harry, tough as he was, would have had to have an army at his back before he would have dared open any attack on this crowd.

After supper, they sat around talking of the coming hunt.

"They say," Harry Crane remarked, "that Quanah Parker's gittin' sore 'bout us hunters takin' off so many buffalo. I heard he's got a new medicine man."

A silence fell as the hunters digested this.

"Now why," wondered Burnett, "did he bring that up?"

It puzzled Burnett. The remark about the Comanche chief didn't fit in with the conversation.

Crude oil lamps and candle gave some

light. They retired early, however. In the dawn they would start their business of hunting buffalo.

And after breakfast One-Shot Harry Crane and his men paid their score, and, saddling up, rode northwest from the Canadian. Nothing had been said concerning the Hide Syndicate, and hardly were the riders out of sight than they were out of mind in the busy preparations.

Chapter XV
Attack

Burnett stuck with Bat Masterson. Both were expert hunters. They did the shooting. Mexican skinners came along after them and brought in the hides to the curing grounds — a flat, grassy stretch two hundred yards from Wright's store.

A small party of Cheyenne Indians rode up during the morning to trade. They left after an hour. Together, with their Sharps remedy, and beltloads of the heavy ammunition the octagonal-barreled greatguns took, the bullets weighing eight to the pound, Vern and Bat rode a couple of miles north of Adobe Walls.

Buffaloes were here, there, and everywhere. They grazed in bunches, from a dozen to a couple of hundred, with varying spaces between them, a few hundred yards at times, a mile at others. Millions stretched north and south over that vast, curled mat of grass.

Spoor was everywhere; coyotes hung on the flanks of the herds, picking up old ones that lay down to die, and also cleaning up after the hunters. That year every coyote in north Texas and Nations grew fat on beef left after the skins were taken. Vultures soared in the sky, waiting.

The two hunters left their horses picketed a mile from the large bunch they decided upon. They stayed down wind, so no scent might be carried to the shaggy beasts. There were bulls and cows, growing calves in the group.

"Ain't any cover to speak of," Vern remarked.

"Nope, but what's the diff?" Bat replied.

At sight of a man on horseback buffaloes would snort and stampede, running madly off, stirring up the surrounding herds. But a man dismounted could get up quite close without the animals displaying the slightest excitement.

Burnett and Masterson started afoot toward the bunch. They came within a half mile of the buffaloes before the creatures showed any uneasiness. A bull tore at the grass with a fore hoof, tossed his horns, sniffing the air, but the wind brought him no warning.

As soon as the two hunters noted this, they flattened out. Then they began to creep up closer. Burnett's brown hand gripped the stock of his Sharps as he dragged it over the grass, muzzle pointed back. A few yards away from Vern was Masterson. Now the animals watched the creeping men with some curiosity but with no alarm at all, evidently considering them some form of coyote.

"B-z-z-z — b-z-z-z!" The rattlesnake's dry warning came to Burnett and Bat. The six-foot rattler was coiled directly ahead of Vern, who pushed his gun barrel out. The touch uncoiled the reptile and it crawled slowly from their path.

Four hundred yards from the bunch Burnett caught Bat's eyes, and when Masterson nodded, Burnett kneeled and raised his rifle to his shoulder. He brought the sights on a spot just behind the bull's foreshoulder, and the great rifle roared. The bull leaped and spread his front legs, blood spurting from his nose. He fought to keep his footing but he was gone. He sank, slowly, rolled over on his ribs.

This bull, taken out by Burnett, was one of the leaders. There was another animal nearby who caught the scent of fresh blood, started toward the prostrate beast, sniffing suspiciously. Before he could sound the alarm Masterson dropped him.

On the slight rise, overlooking the thickly grassed plain where the bunch grazed, they set their rest sticks, and the heavy Sharps began going in earnest. Deep-throated roars of the guns shook the air, but though the buffaloes appeared troubled, and stopped grazing to look around and paw, one after another was dropped.

"Bang!" the Sharps said, and neither man ever missed his kill.

Always killing to windward, they slew about forty head before the blood scent grew so heavy that the remainder of the buffaloes picked up their feet and started away from there.

"Let's make the next stand a mile east," suggested Bat.

In the distance they could hear other roaring explosions, knew their friends were at work. It was not exciting. The stupidity of the buffalo, the crack marksmanship of the hunters, made it simply toil. Back on their horses, they allowed the rifles to cool — too long a period of firing would overheat the Sharps and ruin the barrels.

A Mexican driving a flat wagon, a comrade standing in the rear, came up at their signal, and started to work on the dead carcasses. Expert hands, wielding long, sharp skinning knives, took the shaggy hides off. They were tossed into the wagon.

Vern and Bat went on to their next stand. That first day they each downed fifty buffaloes, a good kill, and returned as the sun was growing red over the vastness of the Staked Plain.

Dusty, tired, shoulders feeling the terrific and repeated blows from the recoil, they rode up to Adobe Walls, turned their horses over to a Mexican wrangler, and stalked inside Hanrahan's saloon.

On the curing ground, hundreds of hides were already staked out. They had been sprinkled with poisoned water to keep off hidebugs and other vermin, the hidebug's object in life being to drill holes in otherwise perfect robes and ruin them. For this the hidebug trailed the buffalo hunters no matter where they went.

Sunlight and salt did the curing. At the end of the killing season, great loads of hides, baled on the flat wagons, would be sent to Ellsworth, Dodge and other settlements, for sale, and shipment to an Eastern market in which every family of any means owned at least one buffalo skin for cover as a carriage or sleigh robe.

Washing up, they forgot the rather monotonous work of the day. Burnett had a drink. Tired of muscle, his brain was not so active and he was able to bury deep within him the thought of Ruth Grey.

Day after day, this life went on, scarcely an event to break the routine. The sun beat hot on the Texas Panhandle; the vultures were thick as swallows in the sky and the coyotes grew so fat they could hardly run out of a man's way. Hunters drifted in and out of Adobe Walls, returning for more ammunition or supplies. Some had their camps far off, moving with the herds.

The June night had been hot as the breath of Hades. Weary from toil, Burnett and a score of other hunters had lain down to sleep on the clay floor of Jim Hanrahan's saloon. They had no pickets out. The Comanches, Cheyennes, Kiowas and Arapahoes had sent in delegations just the previous day to declare their friendship for the white hunters.

Vern Burnett started awake. The light was so faint, as yet, inside the narrow-slotted walls, that it was like night, but he could tell by the bluish rectangle of the open door that the first break of the new day was at hand. Snores and deep breathing came from the other hunters.

Burnett lay for a moment, looking at the door. He was about to go back to sleep again, but once more something startled him to vigilance and Bat Masterson, sleeping next to him, suddenly sat up and rubbed his eyes to clear them.

"What the hell's that?" growled Bat.

His Sharps was already across his legs, and Burnett had his rifle in one hand — the gun lay beside the hunter every night.

Bat came up on his feet, flitted to the door, Burnett at his heels, carrying their guns. Other keen-sensed plainsmen were waking behind them, as the two young fellows peered from the opening.

"Look," Vern growled, pointing with his left hand at the screen of cottonwoods a scant quarter mile away. The trees fringed the banks of the Canadian, and it was to avoid Indians using the river for a screen that Adobe Walls was set in the open plain.

"Yeah, I seen it — Indians!" Masterson replied, and he shouted the last word.

Every man was up, rifle ready. Across the flats from the river tore five hundred mounted, picked fighters — Cheyennes, Comanches, Kiowas, Arapahoes. They came driving at Adobe Walls from the screen of cottonwoods they had used in the approach. War bonnets of eagle feathers flew in the wind of speed, from dark-haired heads. The fierce faces of the savages were twisted with fighting excitement, painted for war. The hairy Indian mustangs were bedecked with ribbons and streamers of white and gay-colored cloths.

Most of them were armed with rifles bought or stolen from whites but many saved their bullets, using the time-honored bow-and-arrows. They made a magnificent charge straight at the tiny settlement, and behind them were a thousand more braves. This was to be a surprise attack and none of the savages whooped.

Bat Masterson slammed the door and dropped the heavy bolts into place. The mud walls were cut by 18-inch loopholes, and from these the hunters made ready to shoot, holding their fire until the enemy was close up.

The score of hunters waited with their buffalo guns. It took the Indians a minute to cross the space from the cottonwoods and Vern Burnett looked them over as they came. No increase of heartbeat excited Vern any more than it did Bat Masterson and his pals. They were so sure of their masterful power that they did not even think of defeat, outnumbered a hundred to one as they were.

"Hear that?" Bat said gruffly.

"Huh, funny. Yuh s'pose this is another of them Mountain Meadows affairs?" Bob Wright growled.

Sounding the charge now, the slamming of the door telling the Indians they had been discovered, came the clear, ringing notes of an Army bugle.

"No Injun could blow like that," Hanrahan drawled, shoving a fresh cud of tobacco into his cheek.

The braves wore round shields of thick buffalo hide, stripped from the shoulders of old bulls, doubled and tripled in thickness. It would stop the bullet from a light rifle. A leading chieftain, a Cheyenne, with quiver of arrows on left shoulder, whipped his right hand toward the quiver. Each time he flashed it away, an arrow came out, feather end in position. With a single motion the arrow went into the string. Drawn to the head, the arrows sang like giant bees at the Adobe Walls' loopholes. So fast was the expert Indian that six or seven arrows were in the air at the same time, one behind the other, before the first struck.

A cloud of arrows fell upon the store, now a fort.

"I'll have the one on the yaller pony, Vern," Bat said casually. "Take yore pick but don't waste lead on mine."

They were together at a loophole, and Jim Hanrahan said: "Now, boys."

Vern Burnett brought a big buck into his sight, caught the thick shield as target. The mass of redskins was upon them.

Chapter XVI
On the Dodge

When the Rio Kid came to, he looked up into a blue sky across which firefly white clouds moved slowly with the south wind. Birds cheeped in the cottonwoods and bushes, and the gentle sound of running water reached his ears. Close by was a blackened, dead fire of buffalo chips, but earth had been thrown over it to kill the smoke, which would show for many miles on the level plains when it was daylight.

"Huh," the Kid grunted.

His head felt sore, his neck stiff. His hand went up, felt a bandage.

"General!"

That was Celestino Mireles. The Mexican youth had been napping close behind Pryor. The sun was warm and beat upon the low trees, which gave them a scant shade overhead, but made a good screen in which to hide.

The soft whinny of a horse came from a nearby grove on the river bank. Saber had heard Pryor's voice, and the dun came pushing up to him, nosed him, trying to make him stand up.

The Rio Kid grinned, patted his pet's velvet nose.

"It's okay, Saber," he told the mustang. "I'm still with yuh."

"He ees like dog, zat fool horse," Mireles observed. "All ze time, General, he act zat way, like he lose bes' frien'. Always he come look at you, try to mak' you get up."

"Where are we. Yuh got anything to eat?"

Mireles brought him some hard bread and a string of dried, jerked antelope meat, a canteen of water.

"We are on ze dodge," the lad told him. "Zees rivaire ees ze Arkansas, we are on beeg bend southeast of Ellsworth."

"What, forty miles from town!"

"*Si,* I dare not stop, General. Shereef Tazewell ees good trailer. Onlee in ze night can I dodge heem. At las' I throw heem off,

166

weend covaire ze trail."

The Kid was munching the food, swallowing liquid, and as he took nourishment he felt fresh strength coming into his body and spirit.

"Yuh shore made a lot of miles in a few hours, Celestino. I was knocked out cold last night, wasn't I?"

"Las' night!" repeated Mireles, staring at him. "General, ees four night' seence you are wounded! Ze pas' days you hav' been — how you call heem — de-leer-i-ous, *si*. I hav' strap you down sometimes."

Bob Pryor started up with an oath. "Four days and nights! What's happened in Ellsworth? How 'bout Grey — Bull McGlon must've had a clear field —"

Mireles shrugged. "Ees nothing I can do, General. I stay wiz you."

"Huh. Wonder if McGlone'd dare touch Ruth!"

The dark eyes of the Mexican narrowed. He was always afraid that his friend might fall in love, settle down somewhere; that would be the end of their riding days together. Snatched from death on the Rio Grande by Captain Bob Pryor, Celestino had come to look upon the life they led as the natural way of existence, grown to love it. Danger was the breath of it but a woman

167

would soon stop that. . . .

"Why," the Kid went on, "Tazewell would stay out, huntin' me for days! Bull'd have a clear field, and unless Fred Grey was mighty careful —"

"We were lucky to es-cape, General," Celestino told him. "McGlone came close to keelin' you. He fire Weenchester, a light bull-et. A Sharps would have feeneesh you. I see you are heet, and manage to get hold of Saber's reins. You hang on weeth knees, zough you were a-sleep all ze time."

The Rio Kid thought for a time, vertical wrinkles between his clear blue eyes.

"I reckon," he drawled, "that McGlone and his chief done won that pot, Celestino. We need a new deal."

He stood up, unsteady, head swimming. Mireles frowned, stepped close to him, steadying him with a brown hand.

"You need more res', General," Celestino cautioned.

"No — I'm okay. We got to ride back, boy, and see how far McGlone's got."

"Eet weel mean death, General. McGlone has ovaire a hundred fighters. Beside, zere's zat shereef."

"Yeah — and Judge Lask and this here Chief behind 'em. I hope Grey and his pards kept themselves barricaded like I told 'em."

Half an hour later the Kid was in the saddle, a bit shaky, Mireles riding beside him, heading north.

It was dark when they saw ahead the glow of the town, roaring with its fun.

They crossed the Smoky Hill west of town, and doubled around, coming in from the northwest. The streets were crowded: Mireles pointed through a narrow byway, said:

"Look, General — zat was Phil Moore's yard. Ees burned."

Blackened ruins on the corner showed where Moore's shack had stood. The big Hide Mart's fence still stood, however. Most of the piled buffalo skins had been saved.

"Grey's house looks okay," growled the Kid.

They pushed toward the mayor's. Lights were on inside, the door was shut. The Rio Kid shoved Saber up to the kitchen entry, and, reaching out, rapped on the panel with the butt of his Colt.

The door opened — and in the portal stood a man, others behind him. For a moment Bob Pryor stared into the hombre's blue eyes; it was almost like looking into a mirror. His upper face was much like the

Rio Kid's, he was of identical size and weight — only his chin spoiled the close resemblance. It fell away, was weak and gave his mouth a flaccid expression. "But," the Kid thought, "with his bandanna pulled up, anybuddy could make the mistake in the dark!" His keen brain instantly guessed that this hombre must be the one, backed by other McGlone gunnies, who had killed and robbed Big Jim Pembroke as the Texas rancher rode back, drunk as a fool, to his cow camp outside Ellsworth.

But there was no time to think things over.

"What yuh want —" began the young fellow, voice a high-pitched drawl.

The Kid would have liked to take him, then and there, but a couple of Bull McGlone's gunnies shoved out into the night.

"Hey — it's the Rio Kid!"

"Bull — hey, Bull, here's that damn marshal!" shrieked the other, digging for his iron.

The Kid put a slug into his guts, folding him up like a jack-knife as his Colt emerged from the holster. Mireles fired an instant later, taking out the one on the right. The man who looked like the Rio Kid bleated in terror, fell grovelling on the floor, yelling: "No — don't kill me, Mister!"

"I wouldn't," muttered Pryor, "not for

anything!"

The floor shook as Bull McGlone, gun in paw, came stamping from up front.

"Chief — hey, Chief, the Kid's back!"

The place swarmed with gunmen, McGlone's aides. From the barn ran more of them, starting for the Rio Kid. Yells rose in the night air. There was not a moment to lose — guns were rising to pin the Kid and his Mexican friend.

Pryor threw bullets into the open doorway. Then he had to whirl on Saber and empty a Colt into the hombres rushing from the barn. They were firing at his moving shadowy shape, and again the Kid heard the shrieks of hatred, the whine of heavy slugs seeking him.

Mireles was ahead of him, turning the corner. The Kid made it, and they spurred madly to the street, cut along the plaza as Bull McGlone called out his fighting men. Horses were grabbed, and armed gunnies spurted on the trail of the Rio Kid.

"There he goes — it's the Rio Kid — take him!"

Men were hoarsely shouting — not only McGlone's followers but some thoughtless citizens, fooled by the planted murder charge against Pryor.

They rode on south, soon left the lighted

area behind; Saber was ahead, Mireles close to him, and they doubled back and forth in the darkness like foxes.

Driven off by enemy guns, the Rio Kid retired southward, across the Smoky Hill. Still weak from his ordeal and the sapping of his strength by the head wound, the Kid went into camp in the bush along the river some miles from Ellsworth.

Dread clutched at his heart, not for himself, but for lovely Ruth Grey. McGlone had taken over Grey's home — where were the mayor and Ruth? Where were Phil Moore and Sam Wilkins, the rest of the Independent dealers?

The gray streak of dawn brought the Rio Kid awake. He came to consciousness again with a start, and his gun, right beside him, as he slept, was in his hand as he sat up, ears alert.

Mireles woke a few moments later, deep-set eyes fixing on the listening figure of his friend.

"What ees, General?" he whispered.

"Hush," warned the Kid. "There's riders comin' through the woods."

Fringes of bush and trees followed the courses of the Kansas rivers, breaking the monotony of the prairie ocean. The Rio Kid, Colt in hand, crept toward the edge.

Their horses were picketed in the thickets, well-hidden.

From the west again came the faint sound of moving horsemen, the dim beat of hoofs, and the crackling of bush. He peeked down the line, and through the interstices of brush sighted the eagle feather headdress of an Indian brave, mounted bare-back on a paint pony. The redskin had a Winchester rifle in one hand and he was engrossed in looking north, at something which the Kid could not yet see, because of an intervening rise.

The amount of dust raised told Pryor that it was a single person. After a few minutes, the rider topped the rise that was between the Kid's hiding-place and the trail.

A startled oath came to Pryor's lips.

The lone rider was Ruth Grey.

Chapter XVII
The Message

Ruth Grey was riding hard, eyes ahead, for the ford across the river.

Quickly Pryor signalled Mireles. The Mexican brought up the Kid's carbine and its heavy belt of ammunition.

"Git yore own rifle, too," whispered Pryor.

"Indians — Cheyennes, I am certain — below."

The two waited. The Kid did not know how many of the savages were lurking in the fringe of woods along the stream. But he soon found out, as Ruth came up.

There were eight of them, and they spurted out, screeching their warwhoops. A couple of them fired arrows over the startled girl, who jerked her mustang's reins, and tried to escape, riding back toward Ellsworth, fifteen miles northeast.

From the cottonwoods, the Rio Kid and Celestino opened fire, lying stretched on the ground, rifles working as fast as they could eject and bring in new shells. Pryor got the chief with his first shot, knocked him sprawling from his paint horse. Mireles downed a flying mustang and finished the rider as the lithe savage hit the prairie, running and trying to swing to face the unexpected threat.

"Got to git 'em all," muttered the Kid. "This might be only a small scouting party, in advance of a large force."

Five were now down. The remaining three turned, trying to escape, having had a stomach full of the brand of fight the Rio Kid and Celestino put up to them. Pryor scrabbled to his feet, ran out into the open.

He knelt, planted a slug between another's shoulders. Mireles brought down a horse, and once again finished the rider. The range was growing long for the carbine, but the Kid fired again and again, covering a pattern with his bullets. He breathed a sigh of relief as the final savage pitched from his running mount and lay still on the plain, within a few yards of the trees.

Whistles brought Saber up. The Rio Kid mounted, galloped after Ruth Grey, who had, through the help of the two in the cottonwoods, made the rise and was running back to civilization.

Topping the rise, the Kid stood high in his stirrups, calling: "Ruth — Ruth!" The wind was with him; the girl heard him and looked back.

A few minutes later the Kid was beside her.

Shock touched his heart. The girl's eyes were no longer as they had been; they were wide with anguish, despair. The color had faded from her young cheeks, and her mouth quivered as she looked at the Rio Kid.

"Bob — Bob!" she said.

She began to cry, and Pryor, shaken to the core, put his arm around her waist to steady her. For moments she sobbed, un-

controllably. Then she pulled herself together, tried to smile at him through her
wet lashes.

"It — it wasn't the Indians," she murmured.

"Where's yore dad?"

That was it, as he had already guessed.

"Dead. He was stabbed to death while he
slept, the night you — the night you —"
She bit her lip, unable to look him in the
eye now.

"The night they say I kilt Pembroke! Ruth,
I never did that shootin'. McGlone fixed up
a man to look like me, and planted me for
the sheriff."

"Bob — I believe you. I — I couldn't take
it in that you'd kill a man for his money
that way, shoot him in the back — it wasn't
you."

"What 'bout Wilkins, Moore, yore dad's
pards?"

She shook her head, sadly. "Moore was
killed the same night. Wilkins, too, I think, I
haven't seen him or several other dealers
since. The ones left have given in to the
Syndicate, and — it's all over."

"Where yuh been since yore dad was
murdered, Ruth?"

"With friends in Ellsworth. I couldn't bear
to stay in the house. In fact, I'm selling it,

cheap, to a man from Texas. Dad had some holdings west of town, along the K.P. I'll let them go, too, for a song. I suppose I'm foolish, but I couldn't stay in Ellsworth any longer. They didn't want me to go, but I took what I had and left, after the funeral. I didn't tell anybody, they'd have tried to stop me. I'm — I'm looking for —" She paused, slowly raised her eyes to his.

"I savvy," he said, voice low, and he patted her hand gently. "I think Vern's gone to 'Dobe Walls, Ruth. He figgered I'd won the deal, and couldn't stand any more, so he lit out. No doubt he's with Bat and Hanrahan. When he comes back, yuh'll see him."

"General," Celestino called sharply, "we stay here and zen we fight not eight but pairhaps eighty Indians!"

"Yuh're right," agreed Pryor. "C'mon, Ruth. I'll see yuh safe to Dodge City. Yuh kin wait there till Burnett gits back from the Panhandle."

They swung, crossed the river, and bit the trail southwest.

It was slow riding. The Kid was in no hurry to get to his destination. He was trying to figure out what to do about Ellsworth, about McGlone and his chief. If they had not done so already, they would, he thought, kill Wilkins, head of the Independents, as they had killed Mayor Grey, also a leader against the Syndicate.

They made camp on the bend of the Arkansas River, up which lay Dodge City, the growing cow metropolis. The railroad had recently come into Dodge, which threatened to supersede Ellsworth. Abilene and other towns in popularity. It was miles closer to the Texas Trail, and offered good facilities for the cattle trade. Colonel Dodge, the railroad builder, had given his name to the new-founded settlement.

They hit Dodge the evening of the second day's ride. The Rio Kid, keeping his chin down in the folds of his bandanna, Stetson low over his eyes, rode in the shadows as far as possible. He knew that Sheriff Tazewell would have sent the alarm for him to the sheriff of Ford County, in which Dodge City stood. And the Syndicate might have agents there who would recognize him.

Ruth had an aunt living in Dodge. The tired, heart-broken girl said good night to the Kid, who left her at the door of the house on the outskirts of the settlement.

Mireles had hung back. Now he came spurring to the Kid's side. "Queeck, General," he said, "push back, out of ze way! Here comes Crane!"

Up the widening street, across the toll

bridge over the Arkansas, rode a bunch of horsemen, in the center of them One-Shot Harry Crane, the Hide Syndicate's chief of hunters. There was a grin on the hard face of the buffalo hunter, burly figure clad in buckskin, Stetson cocked jauntily on his head. Back in the shadows, the Kid and the Mexican watched them pass, dismount and enter the Alamo Saloon.

"Crane looked all-fired pleased with himself," growled the Kid. "C'mon, Celestino, I'm goin' to foller him. Mebbe I kin pay off a little score with one of McGlone's pards."

They dismounted next door to the Alamo, and the Kid, trailed by his friend, walked up on the wide veranda. All windows and doors were wide open, for the night was hot. Dodge was crowded with cowmen and celebrators. The lithe Rio Kid leaned with his back to the wall, close to an open window. Inside, a few feet away, stood Crane with his gunnies strung along the front of the bar.

Crane rang down silver money on the bars, calling loudly: "Set 'em up, barkeeper."

Pryor could, by straining his ears, catch the speech of Crane and his friends.

One-Shot Harry raised his glass of whiskey when it came, remarked with a sneer twist-

179

ing his lips: "Here's to the boys at 'Dobe Walls!'"

The Kid frowned. "Now what's that mean?" he wondered.

It wasn't long until he found out, listening to the talk. A raw-boned devil chuckled.

"When Quanah Parker gits 'em, there won't be enough left to furnish a scrub kiote a meal!"

"Wait'll McGlone hears how I handled it," boasted Crane. "Hanrahan and his bunch won't sell their hides anywheres this season or any other. Quanah said he'd take fifteen hundred braves for the attack. I told him just how to s'prise 'em, 'fore they was awake. And the guns we give 'em cinched the deal!"

Fury gritted the Rio Kid's Teeth. His hand dropped to his Colt and he took a step toward the door, meaning to call Crane and shoot it out on the spot. He could deduce what had happened from the words he had overheard: One-Shot Harry Crane had run ammunition and guns to the Indians of the Panhandle, and sicked them on the hunters at Adobe Walls. He knew Quanah Parker's evil reputation. It would not take much urging to egg the quarrelsome Comanche chief to the attack.

But innate caution gave the Rio Kid

pause. He had no doubt he could down Harry Crane, but if one of the big man's pals got the Kid, or seriously wounded him, it would prevent him from carrying out the rapid plan that was forming in his brain.

Bat Masterson was at Adobe Walls, so was Vern Burnett, and Ruth Grey's future happiness, the Kid knew, depended on Vern. She had made her choice. She admired Pryor and might have loved him had Vern not been in the picture.

The fateful moment passed. Crane and his men had downed their drinks, and were pushing through the whirling crowd inside the big saloon and gambling hall. There were city marshals patrolling the street. Somebody would get hurt in a gunfight.

Now the Kid's chief motive was to attempt to save the men at Adobe Walls. He backed away, found Saber, mounted and rode off to a side street.

"Celestino," he said quickly, "I want yuh to ride to the Fort, and give a letter to the commandin' officer for me. Yuh heard what Crane said, and it'll be a question of getting soldiers down there, and fast. If the s'prise attack didn't take 'em in the first charge, then they'll prob'ly be holed up. They got to have help as soon as it can get there."

In another barroom the Kid obtained a

pencil and a sheet of paper, rapidly wrote off his message. He signed it, "Captain Robert Pryor, formerly U.S. Army."

"Where I meet you?" asked Mireles.

"Yuh'll find me at the 'Dobe Walls when yuh get there with the troopers."

The Rio Kid jerked Saber's rein, the dun pivoted and spurted south for the toll bridge, hoofs drumming hollowly on the boards.

CHAPTER XVIII
SIEGE

As the Indans rushed Adobe Walls. Masterson's Sharps spoke first. He had picked a chief, the one in advance. And with a purpose, he sent his first terrible slug from the buffalo gun right through the center of the buffalo shield. The brave left his mustang, flew through the air, dead before he rolled to a stop two yards from the wall.

"Boy, was he s'prised to find that shield wouldn't stop a bullet!" Bat remarked.

Vern was busy himself. The building was shaken as the hunters sent forth their volley. Fifteen savages, drilled by the heavy long slugs, crashed dead or wounded from their mounts. Ponies, too, went down, kicking and screaming.

Again the besieged group fired, and this smashed the teeth of the charge. The line of warriors split to right and left, flashed by and galloped, shrieking warwhoops, toward the low hills.

"Danged if I ever saw anything like that in my born days," exclaimed Bat Masterson, looking from his loophole.

"Yuh ain't had so many days yit, Bat my lad," Hanrahan said jestingly. "Why, yore razor don't even dull on yore dry beard."

But it was amazing, just the same. Vern Burnett thought so, as he followed Masterson's pointing finger. Up on the hills clustered several hundred other Indians, plainly not in the battle at all.

"They're Osages and Pawnees," Hanrahan growled. "They've come to watch the fun. They won't fight against us, the way their treaty goes."

"Yuh're right," agreed Bat.

It was a strange thing, but Pawnees and Osages did not go on the warpath against the whites. They were simply there as spectators, observers.

Out in the front, in the rising light of the day, the figures of Indians strewed the plain. Vern was watching the one he had hived, watching for a slight movement which might tell him the brave was only shamming death.

"We better block that double door better," Hanrahan said. "Let's pull the rum counter acrost it, boys, and I reckon a spot of breakfast would go good. Way it looks to me, this'll take quite a while."

"Yeah, they got reserves over on the river," Bat agreed. "Must be fourteen or fifteen hundred of 'em altogether, Jim."

Swiftly they worked but no one was showing any perturbation. A Mexican skinner started preparing breakfast.

They had hardly finished their first dispositions of defense when the clear bugle notes rang out again. An Indian, Vern knew, could never blow a bugle like that.

"Here they come again," announced Hanrahan.

The charge, sounded by the bugler came swift and hot. Eight or nine hundred Indians, coming from all sides, made it up, and the buffalo guns roared fury. Steel-tipped arrows struck the mud walls, fell to the earth. Now and then one flew through an opening, cutting a hunter's hair.

Again the terrible, deadly fire of the score of men inside the store smashed the nerve of the charging redskins. They split, rode on out of range, harried by the following bullets of the whites.

Now the Indians gave up those expensive, flamboyant charges. Too many of their number lay dead or writhing in anguish on the flats around Adobe Walls. They returned to the hills, leaped from their ponies, and began shooting with rifles at the rude fort.

The odor of flapjacks and bacon cooking widened the nostrils of the white men, a handful against a red army, inside Adobe Walls.

"Now who says I was a damn fool to waste time diggin' this inside well, boys?" crowed Jim Hanrahan. 'Why, it's real luxury, we don't hafta stir a step outside to git water."

A sentinel went up through the manhole to the roof, lay behind the low bulwark and watched. But the Indians had had enough charging for the moment. They stayed up on the hills and began to fix themselves a meal. Cigars, brought out from Kansas, were passed around among the hunters.

Younger braves were galloping back and forth, although they kept out of close rifle range.

"Wonder how the boys in the store are doin'?" Hanrahan said, mouth full of flapjacks.

Several men had been caught in Wright's. Shots had come from the store's loopholes during the charge.

"I got some cartridges and a long-range-sight rifle in the store," Dixon remarked. "Wisht I had it. We could wake up them young galoots to the folly of showin' off, Bat."

"I'll step over and pick it up and see how the boys are doin'," Bat said.

"I'll cover yuh," Vern promised.

Masterson left his rifle, carrying only his six-guns. He squeezed out through a port-hole in the wall, dropped to the grassy ground. There was a wall of mud between the store and saloon, and Bat started to crawl under the gate. He called loudly to those in the store so they would know he was a friend.

Vern Burnett's rifle roared. He put a bullet into an Indian, who lay dying of his wounds, shamming that he was already through. The redskin had come up on his elbow, taken aim at Bat's back as Masterson headed for the store.

The barred door was opened a crack and Masterson went inside. There were five men in there, and one, young Thurston, lay dying with a bullet in his lungs. He was groaning and begging for water, and there was no well inside the store.

A grizzled old plainsman, "Daddy" Keeler, took a bucket and started for the pump outside, fifty yards out in the open. Though sixty years old, Old Man Keeler was lithe and active. He started out into the open, running swiftly toward the pump. Indians began firing at him, and fifty bullets sped his way. Daddy Keeler reached the pump, and stood up, pumping. Bullets sprayed wood from the pump, and dust flecked up around the old fellow's feet. No man at Adobe Walls would have thought of depriving Keeler of this honor.

His hat was shot off, but he pumped on. Bucket full, Keeler picked up his hat and put it on before starting back. He made the door, and stepped inside, having not spilled a drop of water from the bucket.

"It's shore hot out there in the sun," he said.

All day the pioneers were held inside the Adobe Walls. The Indians showed no signs of retiring. Food was cooked and powwows were held on the domes of the low hills surrounding the camp. They recognized Quanah Parker's distant figure. When dark fell, burial parties stole forth under cover of night. Vern Burnett, a shovel in one hand and rifle in the other, went out to help bury the dead Indians and horses around the buildings. It was a sanitary necessity, for the sun was hot and decay would quickly begin.

There was no night attack. The Indians knew that evil spirits moved in the darkness. During the day, these spirits slept, and then fighting was the thing, but no self-respecting redskin would attack at night.

With a new day came more potshotting, while young braves rode up and down at a respectful distance, shouting and firing at the whites. Heat made the interior like an oven. The acrid powder smoke cloyed the nostrils.

"Looks like we're here to stay, boys," drawled Jim Hanrahan.

"Listen," a young hunter, Dave Kinny exclaimed, "why should we let these red vermin spile our huntin' days, gents? I know what I'm goin' to do. I'm goin' to swipe me a hoss tonight and ride to Fort Dodge. It'll be a lot quicker than waitin' till this convention's over."

"Huh," grunted Hanrahan. "It ain't a course I'd advise, Dave, not if yuh fancy yore hair."

"I kin beat any Indian, runnin' or ridin'," Dave said, and he was not boasting but simply stating a fact.

Kinny rested through the day, while the others played seven-up or worked on equipment to while away the time. No concerted charges were made by the Indians. The spectators still lined the hills, watching with professional interest the siege and various attacks. Smoke of many fires rose on the warm air.

After dark, Kinny squeezed from one of the eighteen-inch loopholes, and crept, a shadow in the night, across the flats. He meant to steal a horse from the picketed mustangs of the Indians. Their own mounts had been stampeded and run off long before by the savages.

The men in the saloon listened for any sounds that might tell of Kinny's discovery by the encircling Indians. It was not until the next morning that Kinny came back to them, tied to the back of a runt mustang. His eyelids had been cut off and his face was a horror. The naked thing on the back of the runt mustang which had been driven to the wall by whooping savages had only agony remaining in this world, the most awful torture had been applied.

Bat Masterson raised his Sharps. He took aim. Marie's long, octagonal barrel never wavered. The gun roared its deep-throated volume and what had been Dave Kinny rose up in its lashings, then relaxed in death. The little mustang, drilled by the same slug which put an end to Kinny's suffering, whirled in circles and rolled over on the plain.

"Dave would have done the same for me," muttered Masterson.

Chapter XIX
Adobe Walls

Cautiously the Rio Kid inched through the underbrush, west on the north bank of the Canadian River. In the distance he could see the dull, thick brown brick sides of the three buildings composing Adobe Walls.

He had left Saber, and though he carried his carbine, belts of ammunition crisscrossing his powerful chest, he had as yet opened no gunfire. On the low domes of hills he could see masses of the Indians, and the scout's keen eyes took in the great array.

Smoke rose from numerous fires. Braves lounged about in their temporary camps, smoking, haranguing. He saw the eagle feathers of chiefs, men who had killed more than five enemies. There were hundreds on hundreds of savages.

Some he could identify: Comanches, Cheyennes, Kiowas from the upper reaches of the Pecos. It was late afternoon, hot as hades. He saw some prostrate, unmoving forms around the walls of Hanrahan's saloon, Indian bodies, dead mustangs, picked off that morn by the marksmen inside.

Now a hundred young braves, anxious to show their lack of fear, mounted on wild, fast mustangs, were lining up for a charge. The Kid started as he heard the clear notes of an Army bugle sounding the charge. The sound was as familiar to him as food and drink, and nostalgia seized upon him. He glanced anxiously around. Obedient as Saber was, the sound of a bugle might bring the dun dashing to answer it.

Sure enough, Saber, unsaddled and untethered, came galloping out as the bugle rang the charge. The dun, his black stripe quivering, mane and tail flying in the breeze, streaked toward Adobe Walls.

The line of Indians rode in mad speed at the tiny outpost, but they did not approach too close, contenting themselves with describing a whooping circle around the buildings, shooting under the necks of their horses, only a foot showing to the hidden men inside. It was with relief that the Kid noted the heavy volley that roared from the loopholes.

"Some of 'em left, anyways," he muttered.

Saber was abreast of his position. The Kid

chanced a quick whistle, hoping to turn the dun. But the heavy gunfire drowned out the sound and Saber galloped on.

A couple of Comanches, fierce faces streaked with war paint, feathers in black hair, naked save for loincloths and bead trimmings, shoved their mustangs out to intercept the swift dun. Though unprepossessing in appearance, the speed of the dun impressed the Indians, and they wondered where the lone horse came from. They swooped down to cut him off.

But Saber caught the scent of them. He hated that smell, and veered south, dodged as they tried to rope him, and galloped off. The two braves streaked after him, and the Rio Kid, watching, smiled as Saber really put on speed and drew away from the chunky, hairy mustangs as though they were standing still.

The boys in the saloon hit several horses, and then got the several Indians dismounted. The savages would lie close behind the quivering forms of their dead mustangs, shooting from walls of flesh. Their comrades, in Indian tradition, tried to pick them up, rescue them, which gave the marksmen more opportunity to kill.

The charge petered out, and the survivors rode back to the hills, where the mighty

Quanah Parker stalked. Powwows were going on. In the golden sunlight, as the day neared its end, the Kid noted the Indians across the way, who seemed to be taking no part in the fighting.

"It's an audience," he decided. "Why, there's hundreds of 'em up there, watchin'! Look like Osages. They're friendly, but interested in the big scrap!"

Not yet did he know that day after day, as the siege went on, the spectators had arrived and taken their places, watching the great fight between the handful of whites and the hordes of Indians under Quanah Parker.

It was a spectacle worth riding a hundred miles to see, in their opinion, but Indian ethics forbade interference with either side.

Saber had eluded his pursuers. He had doubled back east and disappeared in a cloud of dust. Just before the sun fell behind the vast expanse of the Staked Plain, the Kid saw the two who had tried to catch him riding their lathered, weary ponies back to their friends. The dun would not leave the vicinity, but it would take a bullet to stop him. Saber hated Indians, and Indian horses even more.

With the night, the Rio Kid made his decision. He would work in, if possible, and join the men in the saloon. He had several belts of ammunition. They would be able to use another marksman. The cavalry would take longer to make the run from Dodge than had the Kid on his swift dun, and in the meantime he would help his friends.

As soon as it was dark, he started on his belly for Adobe Walls, dragging his carbine after him, inching along, keeping to the screen of cottonwoods along the ragged bank of the Canadian.

With the night the Indians stopped shooting. They would talk till late, around the red fires that popped into glowing vision in the darkness. Braves would recount their exploits, boasting of their prowess and what they would do when they finished the whites inside the fort-like structure.

Dismounted the Rio Kid would, if come upon, be as good as dead. He knew that, but he could move with an Indian's stealth, he had had plenty of such training in the War and afterwards in the wilderness. And to back this, he had a white man's cunning, the brain of a veteran scout.

The time came when he was as close to the saloon as he could make it without leaving his screen. Now he had to cross the clear space surrounding the place. He slowed, making progress across the hot dirt inch by inch, stopping to flatten out, face down. He could hear Indians, stealthy spies scouting around the walls to pick up wounded, though never too close in.

Then he came to the curing grounds. Here were buffalo hides, still pegged out as they had been left when the surprise attack began. The Kid worked one of the hides loose, draped it over his body. It made a good cover under which he might drop when he needed to. He crept on a few yards, then flattened out, still as a corpse.

For nearly half an hour he was forced to stay under the buffalo hide. There was a party of Indians which had crept in, to pick up the body of a chief who had died in the afternoon attack. It took them a long time, for the corpse was uncomfortably near the walls.

When they were gone, the Kid started again. He knew the danger he was in, not only from the savages but from the guns of the whites, his friends. They might shoot him by mistake, in the night.

Slight sounds sent him flat against the earth once more. He lay, not moving a muscle, peeping from under the stinking hide.

Vague shadows showed to him, men slipping from the eighteen-inch loopholes that formed the windows of Adobe Walls. He heard metallic clankings. A burial party was coming out to sink the bodies of dead horses and Indians beneath the dirt. Sanitary precaution made this imperative.

One of them came silently toward the shape that was the Kid, under his robe.

"S-st!" Pryor hailed him, and the man dropped his shovel, gun glinting in his hand.

"Don't shoot — it's a friend," the Kid said quickly.

"What the —" growled the other suspiciously.

Gingerly he approached. The Rio Kid came up on his knees. It was Bat Masterson, and close behind him was Vern Burnett.

"By golly, it's the Rio Kid!" whispered Bat.

Burnett quickly led him to a loophole, and the Kid squeezed through. They had no lights on, but he was greeted in the blackness by Jim Hanrahan. After a time Bat and Vern and the others came in from the burial party, and Hanrahan passed around a bottle of whiskey.

"Damn' if yuh didn't come buffalo huntin' with us, after all," laughed Bat Masterson. "I told yuh it'd be great sport, Bob."

"Some sport," growled Hanrahan, "It's like livin' in an oven in here durin' the day.

Why, I feel like a roast animile."

"Skunk?" jested Bat. "Danged if we're not all beginnin' to smell like it, at that."

"How long yuh been in here?" asked the Kid curiously.

"Ten days now," replied Hanrahan. "Damn 'em, they've spiled this huntin'. Rode all over and cut up our skins and wasted our time and bullets. Lucky I just fetched in supplies from Kansas 'fore they attacked, otherwise we'd be out."

"Help's on the way," Pryor told them. "I sent word to Fort Dodge, gents."

Masterson looked his amazement.

"*You* sent word! How the hell'd yuh savvy we were holed up in here, Bob?"

"One-Shot Harry Crane sorta let me know," drawled Pryor, letting his words sink in.

"Huh? Crane?"

"Yeah. Met up with him in Dodge. He didn't see me but I heard some of his talk with his pards. Seems like he told Quanah Parker yuh had plenty of fresh stuff in here. And Crane give 'em some geegaws to sorta whet their appetites, gents."

"Huh," Hanrahan said. "That's mighty interestin', mighty interestin'. Mighty thoughtful of Crane! As I said, this little party's sorta spiled our hunt, Kid. Nacherly we ain't wastin' no affection on whoever started it. Them Indians is just like children they don't think ahead much. But Crane should've knowed better."

"Yuh're right, Jim," agreed Bat.

Someone touched the Kid's elbow. It was Vern Burnett.

"What were yuh doin' in Dodge, Pryor? Thought yuh was marshal of Ellsworth."

Burnett was crazy to find out about Ruth. Bob Pryor guessed that. The young buffalo hunter would not ask outright, his pride forbade it. Casually the Rio Kid began telling what had happened after the hunting party had left town.

"Far from bein' smashed," he explained, "them sidewinders under McGlone just lay low till yuh boys were on yore way. Then they fixed me up with as neat a frame for murder as I ever heard of. I was run outa town, racin' bullets, by Sheriff Ben Tazewell. Wounded, I come to four days later, my friend Mireles saved me. When I got back to Ellsworth, they'd stabbed Fred Grey daid, took his house, some dummy of McGlone's is buyin' it for a song. They got Wilkins, too, I reckon, and several other dealers who didn't escape or sign up. The Syndicate's sorta called the turn on me, gents."

"Mebbe," drawled Hanrahan, "we oughta sorta sorrowfully remonstrate with this here Crane pusson."

"He only done what McGlone told him to," the Kid said delicately. "I wouldn't blame pore Harry altogether for another's brains."

"Shore, shore. We ain't fergittin' McGlone."

The fingers on the Kid's arm tightened to a steel vise.

"She's all right — she's not hurt," the Kid said quickly. "I mean, Miss Ruth left Ellsworth, I met her ridin' toward Dodge. Took her to an aunt, she's okay."

Burnett's grip relaxed.

"She was," the Kid said to the ceiling, "purty unhappy. It seems somebody done rode away without sayin' good-by, and I dunno as she'll git over it."

Silence greeted this. Then Hanrahan said gruffly: "C'mon, stretch out and git some sleep. We wanta be in shape for the parade when the soldiers prance up, boys. Yuh gab as much as so many old women."

The Rio Kid had ridden day and night to reach Adobe Walls, pausing only to rest Saber so the dun could keep going. His eyes were heavy for lack of sleep. He rolled into a corner against the mud-brick wall and was off the minute his head rested on his folded Stetson, his carbine held in his hand and lying at his side.

He dreamed. He thought he was riding Saber in a cavalry charge, through the hell of cannon and the crashing rifle fire of the Confederates. Bullets whistled past him. He raised his saber, shouting to his men to follow; the bugle sounded the charge. . . .

"At 'em, boys," bellowed the Rio Kid.

He was up on his feet, yelling hoarsely. Yes, and he heard the bugle, but that was all there was of the Army.

Bat Masterson stared curiously at his friend, who was waving his short-nosed carbine in the stuffy, dim air of the saloon.

"Why, he's doin' a dance," Bat drawled, eyes amused. "Cut us another figger, Kid."

The Rio Kid grinned sheepishly. The frontiersmen were at the loop-holes, their Sharps in firing position. Again the bugle's clear notes rang out in the blue-gray dawn. He remembered where he was, besieged with his friends at Adobe Walls.

"Sorta thought I was fightin' again in the Army," he told Bat, and reached for a cup of steaming coffee that stood ready on a table.

"Here they come, they shore are less eager than they were at first," remarked Hanrahan. "I'll take the one on the right, Bermuda."

The Kid gulped down his breakfast, anxious to help break the Indian attack. The Kid's carbine was light for this work. One of those thick-hided buffalo shields would turn its bullet at any distance. But he borrowed a Sharps, and took a stand at one side of a loophole.

Peeking out on an angle to avoid stray arrows or slugs that would come through the openings, the Kid saw Saber come streaking toward the flats. That Army bugle fascinated Saber and he could not resist answering its call.

"Dawgone him, they'll get him sooner or later if he doesn't cut that out," growled the Rio Kid.

"Ain't that yore dun, Kid?" asked Vern Burnett.

"Yep. The fool loves bugles and gunfire, too, though it's the cavalry charge that gits his hoss soul thataway."

Rays of the sun were coming up over the flat horizon. The Rio Kid watched the magnificent charge of the Comanches, the wild riders of the Staked Plain. He took the brave suggested by Billy Ogg, whose peephole he shared, and got his man in the head, killing him instantly. The yelling Indians swerved, and Bat remarked, between roaring of guns: "That's the 'steenth time they've tried it. I reckon they keep hopin' we'll run short of ammunition."

"We will some day," Hanrahan replied. "Pussonally I don't mind a little shootin' practice, gents, but this is gittin' to be tiresome. Business is business, and we're bein' kept from it."

"Thanks to Bull McGlone," the Rio Kid reminded him.

With the first charge over, the new daylight showed the interior more clearly. Pryor looked around. The doors were barricaded, and empty shells lay in heaps around the clay floor. Many of the hunters had slight wounds, but they had lost only two men, young Thurston at the store, and Dave Kinney. The Kid counted eighty Indian topknots, scalps collected by the burial parties when they crept forth at night on sanitary patrol. All these men took scalps, hung them outside where they could dry in the sun, flaunting them in the faces of the enemy.

Food boxes stood around, signs of the long siege — dirtied plates, and tin cups, ammunition, spare guns.

Saber had run very close to the charging redskins. He swerved off again, getting the scent of hated Indian ponies. But several braves had noticed that whenever the bugle blew, the dun would come running. The Rio Kid watched, sweat coming out on his face, as he saw them preparing to capture the fleet dun, his pet and companion through many a long ride.

"They're goin' to try to rope him," Bat Masterson remarked. He knew how Pryor loved his horse. "If they can't, them two lyin' flat'll crease him, Bob."

The distance was long where the party of Comanches, expert judges of horseflesh, made ready to entice the dun. Lariats were coiled and redmen rode into a wide circle, while the Rio Kid, peeking out, caught the sun's glint on the metal bugle. The man who blew it was painted like an Indian and at that distance could not be distinguished from one. He raised the bugle to his lips and began to blow the charge. The clear notes floated through the warming air.

"They'll git him," Bat said. "Look at them two with the rifles, lyin' flat — if the ropers miss, they'll try to stun him with a bullet."

"Damn them," the Rio Kid growled. He threw up his Sharps. But it had buckhorn sights, too coarse for such long-range work.

"Yuh got a gun with fixed sights on it, that'll do decent long-range work?" he demanded.

"Yeah, but it's a long shot, Bob."

Masterson fetched him a Sharps which was equipped with fine target sights. The Kid set himself behind it, tried to gauge the wind velocity and the swell of the land between him and the shining mark that was the Army bugle.

Saber was rapidly galloping in again to answer that call. It was in his blood and he could not resist it. The bugler sat a black-and-white mustang, legs locked to the ribs. Suddenly the Kid's Sharps roared.

Bat Masterson, his eyes on the tiny target that was the horn of the bugle, gave an exclamation.

"Yuh got him, Kid," he cried. "That bugle is shore dented now. Yore slug drove it right down that varmint's throat!"

The black-and-white had spurted from position, came running full-tilt toward the saloon. The erstwhile bugler still sat on the animal's back but he had slumped down, and as he came closer they saw the ruin that had been his face, now a bloody mask. Bat Masterson threw a bullet into the body. The force of it knocked the corpse loose and as the pepper-and-salt bronco swerved, the body fell off and lay quiet on the plain.

Saber, no longer inspired by the bugle's music, caught the scent of the savages, and turned before entering the trap. The braves with the rifles sought to crease him, stun him, but the dun had swung in time and went galloping away in a cloud of dust.

That night the Kid went out with a shovel, and the burial party hunted for the bugler's body. Bat Masterson, scalping knife in hand, sought in vain for something to cut off.

"Why," growled Bat, outraged by the cheat, "this feller ain't got any hair, boys."

"Must be a deserter from the fort," the Rio Kid decided.

"That's it, a buffalo soldier," Bat agreed. "He's bin livin' with the Comanches, no doubt of it. Only he stole that bugle and fetched it with him."

Chapter XX
A Meeting in Dodge

"I'm glad they ain't got any more music," Jim Hanrahan said. "I was gittin' sick of that bugle, it allus played the same tune. That was a nice shot yuh made yestidday, Rio Kid."

They were playing a round of poker, empty shells for chips, whiling away the time between attacks. A sentry, one of their number, stood guard, watching the Indians for their next move.

The hours dragged out, boresome to the active men in the saloon. They had water and food, and plenty of guns and bullets, but their way of life was to keep moving in the open air, and this enforced vacation did not please them. All the time they were losing money, shooting off their valuable ammunition, eating up food they needed in their work, and every day that passed meant they failed to kill hundreds of buffalo.

"I figger," Hanrahan drawled, "that we could each one of us be earnin' 'round two hundred dollars a day. Multiply it by twenty and what yuh got?"

"I dunno," Bat Masterson replied, "but it sounds mighty big, gents. 'Sides, yuh ain't counted what it costs us to keep up this circus."

"Damn McGlone, says I," Billy Ogg snarled. "If ever I —" He shut his grim lips then, and shrugged. His meaning was clear.

The Hide Syndicate had made some dangerous enemies for itself. Had the Hanrahan bunch been wiped out, they might have slept more easily. Or had the Rio Kid not brought them word of who had sicked Quanah Parker on them, again they might have rested peacefully. These men would, perhaps, have looked for another market in which to sell their skins, but it would have been nothing personal as it now had now become.

The long, hot June days dragged on and on, one after the other. It seemed to Bob Pryor that he had been inside Adobe Walls all his life.

"Yuh shore the man yuh sent would git to the fort?" asked Hanrahan of the Kid.

"Shore he would. The soldiers travel slower than I did, boys. They got to have their ammunition train with 'em and other wagons."

"Mebbe they was havin' a big dance and didn't wanta leave," Bat joked, a mischievous light in his eyes.

And yet somehow the days and nights passed. They were all sick of each other's stories, but for the most part there was no friction. Every man at Adobe Walls was a tried and true customer.

On the fifteenth day, the Rio Kid, who was doing his turn as guard while the others whiled away the time at cards, gave a low cry. On the north horizon he saw a snakelike dust cloud that came toward them. It was miles long and rapidly approaching.

"Here they come, boys!"

Intense activity showed among the hostile

Indians. Their scouts were out, and had spied the approaching soldiers. Quanah Parker called off his men. Hundreds had been wounded, and ninety or more lay under the soil around Adobe Walls. The disturbed earth, not yet settled, showed the graves and the topknots drying in the sun, testimony to the beating the handful of buffalo hunters had given the hordes.

Distantly the bugles pierced the warm air. The Rio Kid watched as the war party went scattering down across the shallow waters of the Canadian and galloped south across the Staked Plain.

The audience of Osages and Pawnees came riding toward the Adobe Walls, making the gestures of peace.

A squat Indian chieftain, Black Feather of the sages, slid off his mustang and came to shake Jim Hanrahan's hand.

"How," he greeted, grinning from ear to ear. "Nice fight, heap fine fight." His black eyes, creased in myriad wrinkles, fell on the scalps the white men had taken. He could identify each one, "Comanche" or "Arapahoe," "Kiowa," "Cheyenne!"

The audience fraternized with the hunters, congratulating them. It had been an exciting fortnight, Black Feather insisted, and the Osages were grateful for the circus. The hunters were stretching their legs, glad to be out in the open air of the day again.

Anxiously the Rio Kid searched the plain for Saber, but the dun was not within call. He feared that the Indians might have taken his pet or killed the dun in an attempt to crease him.

Sadly, he watched the United States cavalry come trotting to Adobe Walls. He could make out the lines of troopers, so familiar to him, the guidons flying, and the sunlight on the sabers and carbines.

A captain, a man who had been a second lieutenant in Civil War days and whom Pryor knew slightly, was in the lead, Army Colt in holster, a sword raised in one hand as he led his men. Lieutenants rode out from their platoons.

The blue-uniformed troopers, veterans of the plains and of the Civil War, carried themselves well, though Uncle Sam did not supply them with good horses. Most of the mounts were plugs, and could not hope to overtake the swift Indian mustangs. And Quanah Parker's band was only a cloud of dust on the south horizon when the troopers pulled up.

The Rio Kid thrilled to the sight of the calvalry, his first love. Nostalgia seized him, he remembered the former days of the great fight. Every inch of cavalry accoutrements was familiar to him.

Then he smiled, swore in amusement. Trotting out from the line as an officer's mount should, came Saber, head up, nostrils wide, proud eyes rolling in his head. Though he carried no rider, the dun was cock of the walk and picked up his hoofs daintily as the company wheeled into formation.

Here, too, rode Celestino Mireles, who had carried the Rio Kid's letter to the commandant at Fort Dodge. The slim Mexican youth threw himself from his horse and ran to his friend, grasped his hand.

"General, I theenck we nevaire get here! You are all right, *si?*"

"*Si,*" the Kid told him.

The cavalry captain shook hands with Bob Pryor.

"How in the name of last tarnation did you get down in this God-forsaken hole, Captain?" he asked.

The Kid quickly told him. The captain ordered his men at ease, and then, spurs tinkling, strolled over to Jim Hanrahan who stood close at hand with the beaming Black Feather at his side.

"Say, what was this shindy all about," the captain demanded. "What did you fellows do to rile Quanah Parker?"

Hanrahan shrugged.

"Dunno, 'less it was the color of our complexions," he drawled.

The officer turned to Black Feather.

"Who was in the right, Chief?"

"Why, white man, of course," laughed Black Feather. "Did he not win?"

The hunters held a powwow later on, squatted in a group out in the open air, smoking.

"Well," Hanrahan said slowly, "shall we go on huntin' as though nuthin' had happened, boys?"

The Rio Kid kept his oar out. Bat Masterson spoke up.

"Seems to me," he said, "that I couldn't hunt with no peace of mind, not till I was shore there wouldn't be any further chanct of the Indians bein' riled up to spile our bus'ness."

"Me, too," chimed in Vern Burnett, somber eyes glowing. "I feel the same way. I'm ridin' nawth tonight, gents."

Hanrahan looked around the circle of bronzed, hard faces.

"I reckon Bat's right," the saloon-keeper drawled. "Why, this here Syndicate could pay one tribe after another to use us as arrow targets. After all, we ain't the game, we're the hunters."

Now the Kid spoke up.

"It would be good huntin' 'round Ellsworth, I do b'lieve," he said. "I got a date up there myself."

Guns cooled and cleaned, ammunition belts draped over the horns and strapped across powerful buckskin-clad chests, twenty-two men rode out of Adobe Walls before the sun set. At their head was the Rio Kid, on the mouse-colored dun, and they headed north at a swift clip, bent on vengeance.

They paused, about three days later, at Dodge City, and the Rio Kid led Vern Burnett to the house where he had left Ruth Grey.

It was dusk, and the two young men dropped off their horses and, stiff-legged, stalked up on the porch. The Kid knocked and a middle-aged, full-bodied woman answered.

She stared at the dust-covered pair, and frowned. "Now what do you two want?" she asked.

"Please, Ma'am," the Kid told her, sweeping off his Stetson to bow gallantly, "yuh must remember me, Bob Pryor. I fetched Miss Ruth Grey here some days ago."

"Oh — Bob!"

Ruth Grey had heard the Kid's voice. She

came streaking from the parlor, and she was so glad to see Pryor that she reached up and kissed him.

Vern Burnett stood on the porch still in the shadows. The girl's anxious eyes were filled with the lamplight, and she was looking up into the face of the Rio Kid.

"Did you — have you — where is he —" she stammered.

The Rio Kid grinned, stood aside. He reached out, and pulled Vern Burnett into the hall. Then Ruth, after a quick look at her sweetheart, dropped her gaze. Vern, the blood flushing up under his tanned, smooth cheeks, nearly tore his Stetson brim to pieces with his agitated hands.

"Ruth," he muttered, "I — I come back."

Aunt Nelly, Ruth's mother's sister, said pertly: "So we see, young man. Ruth, is this the fellow who ran away from you?" She glared at Vern, who was in a dither of embarrassment.

The Rio Kid laughed. He crooked his arm, bowed and offered it to Aunt Nelly. "S'pose, Ma'am," he suggested, "we go find us a drink. It's bin a mighty dry summer."

Aunt Nelly could take a hint and she also took the gallant Rio Kid's proffered arm, leaving the lovers alone.

Chapter XXI
Revenge Is Sweet

The day had been dryly hot, sun beating relentlessly on the dry plains and the roofs of Ellsworth's buildings. The town seemed deserted. Citizens stayed in the shade, taking it easy, napping out the hot afternoon hours.

A dilapidated wagon with a black body, a light rig drawn by a sleepy mule, creaked slowly along Douglas Street, heading toward wide Main, split by the Kansas Pacific tracks. On the seat, ahead of the enclosed section, slouched a Mexican lad, chin sunk on breast, steeple sombrero with silver conchas screening his head and upper trunk with its wide brim.

Inside the confined space of the wagon body, the Rio Kid peeked from a hole, taking in the central part of town.

"Is she clear, Kid?" asked Bat Masterson, squeezed in another corner, his Sharps buffalo gun in hand.

"Shore looks so," Pryor replied. "I don't reckon they expected us back so soon."

"If at all," growled Jim Hanrahan, also hidden in the wagon.

This was the opening of the Rio Kid's strategic blow against Bull McGlone's Hide

Syndicate. Bent on blood revenge, the score of buffalo hunters had made a record run from Adobe Walls. Split up into groups of two or three, the rest of them were converging on the town, ready to gallop in at the Kid's signal.

The three leaders meant to get to the heart of the Syndicate before their presence was discovered. McGlone would never expect them so soon, if at all.

"Le's git it all straight, for the last time, Kid," Bat Masterson said, as Celestino Mireles, who was driving the wagon, swung the corner onto Main Street. "Hanrahan and you are openin' at the Syndicate office. Yuh want me to take what used to be Grey's house."

"Yeah," said Pryor. "And be shore, like I told yuh 'fore we started in, that yuh don't kill the young feller who looks like me from the mouth up. Yuh tend to him yoreself, Bat. I got to have him alive. And don't forget Bull McGlone is mine!"

"Right," Hanrahan agreed. "McGlone's yores if yuh kin git him. But if any of the boys sight One-Shot Crane, I guarantee nuthin'."

"I figger," the Kid told them, "mebee that weak-chinned hombre kin tell us who's bin backin' McGlone. There's Jedge Lask, and if there's anything I hate it's a slick crook like him."

"Me, too," chimed in Bat. "Well, here we go, Kid. Good shootin' now."

They looked to their guns in the dim interior. Sifting toward Ellsworth they knew their friends, on horseback, were drawing close, ready to charge when the ball opened.

The Rio Kid, being an outlaw in Ellsworth, had thus masked his entry into town. He wished to gain the heart of the settlement before being recognized, since he was fair game for any deputy or citizen who should spy him.

Down the K.P. tracks a puffy, self-important little switching engine was restlessly changing the positions of strings of cattle cars.

Over what had been Phil Moore's Hide Mart hung a newly painted, large sign. A shack of boards had been thrown up, and the fenced yard was piled roof-high with buffalo hides, loot of the Syndicate.

The Kid, from his peephole in the side of the wagon, took in the new sign: "KANSAS HIDE SYNDICATE. J. T. McGLONE, PRES. BEST PRICES FOR SKINS."

"Here we go," the Rio Kid said softly.

Jim Hanrahan grunted in satisfaction.

The yard gate was closed, but there were several gunnies lounging on a wide bench at the shady side of the porch, the shack's front door opening on Main Street, the yard extending down the side way.

Mireles, screened by his gigantic sombrero, pulled the mule to a halt and the beast at once went to sleep.

The Rio Kid pushed open the back panel of the wagon and jumped to the dusty earth, Hanrahan behind him, then Masterson. They were up on the low veranda before the gunnies saw them, while Bat streaked across for Grey's former abode.

Horsemen started in from the alleys between buildings. The door into the "Office" stood wide open, seeking what air there was. One of McGlone's Texas gunmen opened his eyes, saw the Rio Kid and Jim Hanrahan.

"Hey!" he shrieked.

Electrified men leaped to their feet, diving for their guns, but Hanrahan and the Kid jumped inside and slammed the door. Mireles had hopped down from his box, taken cover behind the wagon, and half a dozen of the buffalo hunters came spurring up, their rifles and pistols blasting the handful of Syndicate men in front.

The big shack was divided into a front and rear section by a partition which reached nearly to the ceiling. At a flat oak desk, back to the wall, Bull McGlone sat, leaning back in his chair with his feet on the top of the desk. The big fellow had been taking a nap. He wore elegant duds, black silk shirt, black pants, and hundred-dollar boots. Nebraska Bull, "President" of the Syndicate, had turned dandy with his new position.

The confused shouts, the opening shots, startled McGlone awake. He had been drinking heavily the night before and was sluggish. Red-flecked eyes blinked at either side of the squashed nose, thick-lipped, sullen mouth dropping open as he took in Bob Pryor and Jim Hanrahan, whom he believed to be dead, massacred at Adobe Walls.

The giant sniffed, one side of his mouth flickin gup.

"Why — howdy, boys," he growled, with forced heartiness. "Glad yuh're back — what kin I do for yuh?"

The Rio Kid caught his quick glance at the portal between rooms.

"Watch that door, Jim," he ordered.

Hanrahan glided over into position, on the way slapping Bull McGlone in the mouth with the full force of his horny hand.

"Damn yuh," McGlone snarled. "What yuh come here for?"

"We come to trade hides, ours or yores," announced the Rio Kid sternly. He stood, no guns in his hands, feet wide, paces from Bull McGlone. "Go for yore Colt, Bull. It's yore last draw!"

McGlone's feet had thudded to the floor when Hanrahan hit him. A trickle of blood slowly coursed down the jutting chin, blue with beard stubble. But he did not move, fear burned in his eyes, for he had seen the speed of the Rio Kid's draw.

"What the hell —" That was One-Shot Harry Crane, the Hide Syndicate's chief of hunters, the man who had carried out the cunning plan to sick Quanah Parker on Adobe Walls. The burly Crane loomed in the opening between the two sections of the shack.

Explosions were increasing in the street, Sharps roaring their deep-throated tones. The whiplike crack of Winchesters made the treble accompaniment while Colt revolvers barked. The battle was opening.

Only seconds, instants in the eternity of time, had elapsed since Hanrahan and the Kid had stepped into McGlone's office. Behind Harry Crane crowded a dozen hired retainers.

Crane was a man of action. He guessed, from the look of Jim Hanrahan's grim, fierce face, from the Rio Kid's stance, that the jig was up and it was gun to gun.

Crane was swift and his draw was that of a veteran. He went into shooting crouch, and his pistol exploded, booming with ear-splitting reverberations in the confined space of the office. His slug kicked up splinters at Jim Hanrahan's feet. With a pleased smile on his lips, Jim Hanrahan shot Crane through the heart and the burly buffalo hunter folded up.

A roar of rage yipped from the rear room, Hanrahan peppered the entry with bullets, and smoke rose acrid to the spread nostrils of fighting men.

In the meantime Bull McGlone grasped the slight advantage, the confusion afforded him. He, too, knew this visitation meant life or death. He had, in case any disgruntled dealer or hunter put up an argument, made preparations: nailed by his knee, under the desk, was a holster and in the holster a spare pistol. He had taken care that his hands should come down beneath the desk when his chair plunked to the floor. He let go, shooting under the desk top. His first bullet tore a chunk from the outer edge of the wood and drilled the Rio Kid's leather-covered thigh, ripping out a chunk of flesh and passing on, plugging into the wall. The angle was difficult.

McGlone, the moment he made his shot, fell out of his chair, ducking behind the thick oak slab. He was raising his gun for better aim. The Rio Kid braced himself and made his rapid, lightning draw, long-barreled Colt emerging from its pliant holster with the speed of legerdemain. He had just an instant-fraction, while McGlone's ugly face showed level with the desk top as the giant dropped. In that tiny bit of time the Kid made his shot, and his .45 slug smashed into the man's squashed nose and drove through to his brain.

Nebraska Bull McGlone rolled under the desk, dead.

They had the two leaders. They began the mass battle against the Syndicate gunmen, hired killers brought in from several states by McGlone. Hanrahan and the Kid took the thick desk, and each having a side began firing at the bunch in the door. Fast as chain lightning, cool in action, neither missed his kill. Every slug hit a man, mortally wounding or killing. Inside of a minute the doorway was a welter of death, bodies piled waist high, and the gunnies left had had a bellyful of it.

Blood showed on Hanrahan's leathery cheek, but he shifted his cud of tobacco to the other side and kept right on chewing steadily, eyes never showing the slightest excitement. The Kid came up erect. It hurt him to walk, but he lurched for the inner door, blasting the other room with his guns.

The remnant of gunmen who had been in there were taking to the windows and hustling from the door. The Kid hived them out, and Hanrahan at his heels, stepped into the sunlight.

He was out in the hide yard around which a fence had been built, and behind this cover were fifty or sixty of the Syndicate's men who had been sleeping off the night before in the shade of the stacks. They were fighting the buffalo hunters in the street, and Hanrahan and the Kid saw their golden opportunity.

Squatting back in the doorway, the two began to rake the rear of the enemy line. One after another their Colts roared death to the killers. They downed a dozen and wounded as many more, when their heart-breaking shooting stampeded the hired gunnies, and sent them running for their horses and escape from Ellsworth.

Across the wide street and the tracks, Bat Masterson was at work. A few gunshots rose from the former mayor's home, but they were lost in the crashing volleys around the Syndicate's quarters. Confusion dominated the yard, and like magic the fences cleared of fighting men, gunnies scattering every which way.

There were stables down the side street, and a corral in which their horses were kept. The gunnies were headed for their mounts, but as they appeared from behind the fence, expert marksmen who had their cover behind posts and walls, picked them off. About half of the gang made the corral, while the Rio Kid sang out to his friends: "Get yore mounts, boys — there they go."

He dashed back through the building, hurdled the pile of bodies in the door, and issued into the street. Saber was saddled, his reins held in Celestino Mireles' brown hands. The dun had been brought in by the other hunters.

"General — you are hurt," Mireles cried, seeing the Kid's lurching gait.

"Nothin' to worry about," the Kid replied, leaping into his leather.

As he spurred to the corner he glanced across the way. He saw Bat Masterson was on the porch of Fred Grey's house. Several hombres were being lined up, hands in the air.

Now Ellsworth was waking up to the fact that there was something happening.

People taking siestas came to their windows. The town marshals rushed out, shotguns in hands, rubbing sleep from their eyes.

About fifty of McGlone's fighting men, in bunches strung out behind each other, had hit the saddle and were riding hell-for-leather south out of Ellsworth. Behind them came fifteen buffalo hunters, and Saber carried the Rio Kid out in the van.

Their leaders gone, the gunnies were heading for the Texas Trail and the wilds of the Indian Nations, panic in their black hearts.

A gunny lieutenant saw how things were going; he sought to rally his men. "This way, boys," he howled, emptying his gun back at the Rio Kid. "C'mon, stick together — fast ones wait up for the slow ones —" By arm motions and with his quirt, he managed to round up thirty of the fleeing fighters, quickly threw them into circle formation, facing outward in all directions.

The Rio Kid gave a shrill warwhoop. Old Man Keeler, earnestly flogging his lathered mustang up, Bermuda Carlisle, Billy Ogg, Andy Johnson, and the others took it up.

"Let's show 'em how they done it at 'Dobe Walls, boys," Hanrahan roared.

He began riding a fast circle, leaning off his horse, firing into the bunched gunnies under his mustang's neck. With grins on their bearded faces, the buffalo hunters accepted the grim jest. They rode with a boot showing for a mark to the rattled killers in the center of their loop.

Spurring madly in a wide ring on Saber's back, the Rio Kid smiled with the reckless abandon of battle. They had divided the gunnies in half within the first few volleys; the remaining ones were trying to imitate the hunters, staying behind their horses, for there was no cover on the flat, broad plain where they had been overtaken.

Indian fashion, the buffalo men rode, their warwhoops terrifying. Each shot made its hit, killing or wounding, or throwing more fear into the syndicate hirelings.

Suddenly a gunny thrust up a white rag, a chunk of shirt he had torn from his clothing. Guns were thrown out, glinting in the afternoon sunlight.

The shooting stopped. The smashed remnants of hombres who had fought for the Hide Syndicate stared in fascinated terror at the terrible fighting men who drew upon them.

"Hey, Kid, there's a few got away. S'pose we leave these softies with Keeler and the boys and me'n yuh go after 'em," suggested Hanrahan.

The hunter had a powerful horse under him, uninjured. Saber was fresh enough, and the Rio Kid nodded. Guns refilled, they spurred south on the trail of a half dozen who had managed to outride the avengers of Adobe Walls.

Three escaped together. Hanrahan and the Kid rode the others down two hours later, on the Trail south of Ellsworth.

Slowly the two cantered the foam-covered horses back for town. The sun was a tremendous red ball to their left as they splashed through the river and turned into Ellsworth. Night was close.

The Rio Kid walked the dust-covered dun up the center of Main Street, in full sight of the citizenry. Men were out, and there was high excitement in Ellsworth as word of the big fight, the smashing of McGlone's Hide Syndicate, spread like wildfire from lip to lip. So fast had been the blows struck by the buffalo hunters that the scrap was done before anybody got into action.

Happy Jack Morco stepped off the walk, ducked under a hitch rail, and came toward the Rio Kid and Harahan.

"Hey, there, Pryor! Listen, there's a warrant for murder out for yuh. I got to do my

226

duty. Don't blame me but —"

Chapter XXII
The Chief

"Shut up!" Hanrahan growled, eyeing Morco with such a scowl that the marshal blinked and said quickly:

"No hard feelin's, Jim. Honest, Jedge Lask says we got to take Bob, dead or alive —"

The Rio Kid laughed. "I'd sorta forgotten Lask."

"Tell yuh what, Jack," Hanrahan said. "Yuh go find us a barrel of tar and a bag of feathers and then we'll talk 'bout the Kid surrenderin'."

"I'll let yuh arrest me pretty pronto," promised Pryor. "Just now there's things I got to do, Morco."

They trotted past the marshal. Happy Jack was loath to open fire on them, for they were friends, and they were two of the best shots in Kansas.

"Mebbe the jedge made a mistake, at that," he muttered.

Bat Masterson had charge at Grey's house. A couple of the hunters were with him, guns herding half a dozen prisoners into a corner. The others, thirsty from their hard ride north, and bored now the scrap was over, had gone to visit various oases.

"Here's the man yuh wanted, Kid," Bat said, shoving forward the chinless wonder Pryor had seen when he had ridden up to the back door the night he had returned to town after the frame-up. "I spotted him right off, he's shore a ringer for yuh, 'cept for the chin and mouth. Says his name is Tip Hanson and he's from Hays."

Tip Hanson was in mortal terror of Bat Masterson. His blue eyes fell before the stern frown of the Rio Kid; a guilty look flushed his cheeks.

"Any of our dealer friends around?" inquired the Kid.

"Yeah, I seen a few, Kid. All of 'em either quit, or run, those the Syndicate didn't kill. Met Sam Wilkins. He told me he was in the real estate game now, the Syndicate skeered him out."

"I thought Wilkins was done for," the Kid growled.

He swung on Tip Hanson, drilled him to the core with his hard eyes.

"What — what yuh want of me, Mister?" demanded Hanson.

The Rio Kid seized him by the shirt front, yanked him roughly around, jammed him against the wall. He began to shoot accusations and questions at Tip Hanson.

"Hanson, listen to me — McGlone fetched yuh here to frame a murder on me. Yuh waylaid Big Jim Pembroke that night outside town while he was ridin' home drunk with a couple of his cowboys. Back in the shadows were more of yore pards, McGlone's gunnies. They called to yuh, namin' yuh the Rio Kid! Yuh shot Pembroke dead, and robbed him. McGlone's men gunned the cowboys, not killin' 'em but wishin' 'em to act as witnesses against me. McGlone planted Pembroke's roll in my bunk at the Grand Central — and now yuh're goin' to tell the town the real truth!"

Tip Hanson gulped with terror. His eyes rolled in his head and his teeth rattled as the Rio Kid shook him.

"Aw right — I on'y done what McGlone said — I hadda," he gasped.

Bat Masterson looked out the window. From the plaza came the sound of a crowd collecting.

"Hey, there's Lask, he's makin' a speech," Masterson exclaimed.

"I wanta talk to this skunk a while longer, Bat. I'll join yuh in a few minutes," the Kid promised.

Ten minutes later he strode toward the people who were listening to Judge Newbold Lask, standing on a wagon in front of the courthouse. Vern Burnett slouched over to the Kid, who thrust Tip Hanson into the tall buffalo hunter's hands.

"Hold this for me, Vern."

The Rio Kid walked, hands swinging easily at his sides, straight toward the crooked judge.

He shoved a way through the crowd. The huge Burnett, practically carrying the unnerved Tip Hanson, followed. He was nearly upon Lask when the judge caught sight of him, recognized him. Lask paused for an instant, gulped, and then pointed a long finger at the Kid.

"There he strolls," Lask shouted furiously, face red as a beet. "The murderer deluxe, the Rio Kid! Gentlemen, I am usually in favor of allowing the law to take its course, but in some cases, and I say to you that this is most surely one, the law needs a little help from decent men! There's a warrant for this killer's arrest in Marshal Morco's pocket right now, but he dare not serve it because this devilish murderer from the Texas hinterland would slay him! Do your duty, citizens — seize this man, string him up!"

Lask fairly shrieked the last words of his inflammatory speech.

The Rio Kid was at the end of the flat wagon on which Lask stood. There were many people in Ellsworth who had been fooled by the machinations of the Syndicate and its slimy chief. There were many who believed implicitly that Bob Pryor had killed Pembroke.

"Git a rope!" someone yelled.

The Kid jumped up on the wagon.

"Gents," he cried, "I got someone here who wishes to tell yuh the truth for a change —" Pryor signaled Burnett.

Vern hoisted up the trembling Hanson.

"Make yore talk, Hanson," ordered Pryor.

Tip Hanson stared at the sea of excited, angry faces. He gulped. Then he felt the stirring Colt muzzle the Rio Kid prodded him with. As he spoke, quiet fell over the gathering.

"I — I done shot Pembroke that night," he whimpered. "Bull McGlone made me do it 'cause I — I look like the Rio Kid. McGlone planted that roll under Pryor's mattress — they wanted him done for. Lask — Lask was s'posed to hold him, then we was goin' to — to lynch him —"

As he paused, the Kid reached from behind Hanson and pulled the hombre's bandanna up over his mouth. He stood alongside the killer, and a man up front

231

cried, "Why, they're like as two peas, that-away!"

Pryor shoved down the mask; Hanson's weak mouth quivered with fright.

"Who's the man behind all this? Who bribed Lask and hired McGlone and planned the ruin of the Kansas hide dealers?" shouted Pryor.

"Wilkins — Sam Wilkins!" wailed Tip Hanson. "He done it all, worked it out."

"Well, damn my hide," gasped Bat Masterson. "He shore had me fooled. Why, I met him this afternoon and let him go —"

"It was Wilkins, gents," the Kid explained. "Hanson's told me the hull dirty tale. Wilkins posed as a friend of the independent dealers, was even elected their head. That's the way the Syndicate got its inside information. Wilkins had robbed and killed — he stabbed Fred Grey to death, enterin' Grey's home as a friend. And he's bought himself thousands of acres of new town sites along the Kansas Pacific, west of here. That'll make him the richest man in Kansas. He did this with money he stole from dealers and cheated their families out of. Yuh can git some of this back, and help make up some to those left behind —"

"Watch it, Kid —" That was Bat Masterson, and his .45 flew into his hand but he dared not shoot — the Rio Kid was between Judge Newbold Lask and Bat's gun.

The Kid whirled. Lask had drawn a small derringer from inside his ruffled waistcoat. The popgun snapped, and the Kid felt the sting as he turned. His movement made the little slug miss his head and it bit a piece from one ear.

An instant later the Rio Kid had Lask's thin wrist in a grip of steel, and the derringer tinkled to the wagon floor.

"Lynch him — string Lash up!" somebody yelled.

Jim Hanrahan sprang to the wagon.

"No, gents, I got a better idea," the big buffalo hunter roared. "I done put in an order for a barrel of tar and a bag of feathers when we hit Ellsworth. It's right under that shed!"

Catcalls and laughter rose. The deadly mood of the crowd changed. Lask was laid hold of; his clothes were torn from his body as he fought, cursing them. The thieving judge, a crony of Sam Wilkins, chief of the deceased Hide Syndicate, was paying for his betrayal of trust.

A few minutes later the figure of Judge Lask, sitting a fence rail, rode out of Ellsworth. Black tar had been smeared over him, and white feathers stuck to the viscous liquid.

The Rio Kid signaled Masterson.

"I'm in a hurry, Bat," he said. "Take charge, will yuh? Turn Hanson over to Morco and Hogue. I got to be ridin'."

"Don't yuh want some help?" asked Bat.

"Not this time," smiled the Rio Kid. "He's gone to Nauchville, Hanson says. If he ain't there, I'll foller him to hell."

On the dun, trailed by Celestino Mireles, the Rio Kid covered the half mile to Nauchville in a burst of speed. This time he rode to the garish front door of the Blue Buffalo, and shoved through the batwing, the Mexican lad covering his back.

The front was filled with riffraff, crimson women and crooked gamblers, their drunken victims. The Kid strolled through to the back. The door was locked, and he put his shoulder against it, broke through.

Wilkins sat there, at the wooden table in the rear room. He knew his time was up. Judge Lask had been his last hope, his final devilish play. He would not leave the fortune he had stolen from decent Kansans, and he was drowning what he felt in whiskey.

"So yuh don't drink," sneered Pryor, standing just inside the door.

His hands hung loose at his narrow, gun-circled hips.

The aspect of florid Sam Wilkins was so different from the easy-going, apparently good-natured hombre who had posed as head of the Independent dealers that the Rio Kid hardly knew him. Wilkins was sitting bolt upright in his chair. His hands gripped the edge of the table with such force that his knuckles showed white.

Black fury, the hate and poisonous rage he felt, crimsoned the chief's drawn face. The oil lamp guttered, smoking against the glass chimney, to his left. At his right lay a Colt revolver, and in front of him was the half emptied bottle of whiskey, into which Wilkins stared as though hypnotized.

"Wilkins!" snapped the Rio Kid.

This time his voice seemed to penetrate the inward shell into which the chief had drawn. Slowly Wilkins raised his hot eyes and looked straight into the cold blue orbs of the Rio Kid.

"Damn your soul, Pryor," Wilkins said flatly.

A cold feeling ran up the Kid's spine. He had looked on rattlesnakes, on bad men galore, on looters in the army, and the lowest of the low, but this terrible hombre was the nastiest he had ever come upon.

"You're under arrest, Wilkins."

"No," Wilkins declared.

He shifted, but as the Kid hoped he would go for his gun, Wilkins picked up the bottle of whiskey and raised it to his wet lips. He threw back his head and drained the entire bottle.

Then he cursed and flung the heavy flask at Pryor's face. It whirled, turning in the air. The lithe, agile Kid stepped quickly aside, the bottle brushing against his cheek and smashing against the wall.

As the eyes of the Kid involuntarily followed the scintillating glass in its flight, Sam Wilkins went for the Colt at his hand.

He fired, teeth gritted in his hate. The Rio Kid felt the slug tear through his shirt and vest, burn his side, inches from his heart. The hand that manipulated the gun was lax from whiskey, and Pryor's gun, flashing out in one streaking play, boomed a reply as Wilkins took steadier aim.

He shot to kill. Wilkins would never surrender. Another bullet at such close range might get the Kid —

Between the fierce, red-rimmed eyes of Sam Wilkins appeared a blue hole, the mark of the Rio Kid's bullet. It drove through the evil brain, emerged from his brick-colored head above his ear and hit the board wall with a dull thud.

For an instant Wilkins sat there, bolt upright, then the hand holding his gun collapsed, his muscles went limp, and he fell forward, dead, on the table.

Almost retching, the Rio Kid swung on his spurs, and walked out through the saloon; a tinny piano banged out a lilting tune.

"Come, General, ees time we ride," Celestino begged.

The Rio Kid, who had been best man at the wedding of Vern Burnett and Ruth Grey, who had recovered for them and others a great deal of the wealth stolen by Wilkins, stared down into the soft, smiling eyes of the young woman. She clung to Vern's stalwart arm, and Burnett reached up to shake the Kid's hand.

Vern Burnett's eyes no longer held that somber glow; the powerful young buffalo hunter had found happiness.

"We'll be settin' up in the hide business, Bob," Vern told him. "Reckon we'll stay here in Ellsworth. And remember, our teepee's the same as yore own."

The Kid smiled. He leaned down, kissed Ruth Grey on the lips.

"*Adios,* and good luck," he said. "We're headin' for acrost the Pecos."

He swung Saber. Equipment burnished to

army perfection, clothes and guns in strict order, the Rio Kid swung south out of Ellsworth.

Once he turned to look back over his shoulders. Ruth Grey waved to him, Burnett holding her with his strong arm.

"Might be me standin' there," he mused, "if —"

Then he shrugged, and a smile lightened his handsome face. He was on the trail again, restless, but footloose and fancy free, ready to fight greed and evil once more and to bring peace and justice wherever they were needed.